★ "A magnificent achievement, one of the really out-standing young adult novels of this decade—or any for that matter."

—STARRED/*The Horn Book*

"A fascinating historical novel . . . Newth's writing, even in translation, is intensely lovely."

—Suzanne Curley, *Newsday*

★ "Riveting, thought-provoking, and demanding."

—STARRED/*School Library Journal*

♦ "A harrowing but finely wrought reconstruction of cruel events unfamiliar to most Americans."

—POINTER/*Kirkus Reviews*

An ALA Best Book for Young Adults
A *School Library Journal* Best Book of the Year

The Abduction

Mette Newth

The Abduction

Translated from the Norwegian by
Tiina Nunnally and Steve Murray

aerial fiction
Farrar, Straus & Giroux

Item:

> *wee doe not thinke it good you should*
> *bringe hither above the number of 8 or*
> *tenne at the most of the people of that*
> *countrie. Whereof some to be oulde and the*
> *other younge whome wee mynd shall not*
> *return agayne thither.*

—Instructions of Queen Elizabeth I of England
to Captain Martin Frobisher
before his expedition to Greenland, 1577

The Abduction

There was once a world before this one,
and people lived there
who were not of our lineage.
But the pillars of the world collapsed,
and everything was turned into nothingness.
And the world was emptiness.
Then two men were formed
out of small mounds of earth.
They were newborn and fully grown at the same time.
And they wished for a child.
A powerful song transformed one of them into a woman,
and they had a child.
They were our first ancestors,
and from them all lands were populated.

                              Tuglik, Igloolik, 1922

4]

*T*he snow retreated reluctantly from the slopes of the mountains.

Clouds heavy with rain hastened across the sky. Shadows, like long dark fingers, drew somber traces on the glowing colors of the mountainsides. One brief moment and then the clouds drifted on, and the icebergs at the mouth of the fjord were once again bathed in the dazzling light of the spring sun.

The wind came from the inland ice cap, warm as the breath of an eager young hunter. It broke up the winter ice in the bay and once again set free the forces of the ocean current.

In only a few days, long cracks had appeared in the ice and revealed dark, living water.

It was time for summer journeys and hunting for the winter.

The longhouses lay sheltered in the hollow between the mountains, almost as if they had sprouted from the hillside. Thick, rough walls of stone and soft sod roofs. With their long, tunnel-shaped entrances they kept out the icy cold in the winter and held in the heat from the oil lamps. They faced the shore, the bay, and the endlessly sailing icebergs sent forth by the inland ice cap.

Spring wind and sunshine. Spring wind and rain. Time for departures and changes.

Osuqo knew that this time the spring wind was the sign of the greatest change of all, from child to woman.

From clean to unclean.

Her body told her that the changes were near. Her mother had known it for a long time.

"The time has come. Your body will release the unclean blood which shows that you are fertile. You will take your place among us women and observe the laws carefully, so that the souls of the animals will not be harmed and the men's hunting will not be poor."

Osuqo was sitting with the other women on the doorsteps outside the longhouses. Around them lay the summer tents, the hunting implements, and the kayaks. Heads bowed, hands working on new rips, seams that had torn open, worn-out strips of hide.

Osuqo's thoughts circled around the laws that she knew so well but now would have to observe so carefully. Now it was also her responsibility to make sure that the laws were not broken, so that the whale, the seal, and the polar bear would not stay away from the hunting grounds.

It was a great responsibility. She felt grownup. Even though the unclean blood had still only flowed for the first time.

Head bowed, hands idle.

Her thoughts were frightening and comforting at the same time. Good to belong, but so much to handle alone.

The women were talking about everything that had to be done for the summer journey. The roofs of the longhouses had to be lifted off so that the sun, the spring wind, and the rain could clean the houses before the winter. Heavy work, of course. But so much was done by nature itself.

The women's boats and the kayaks. Every one of the triple-layered, watertight seams had to be examined carefully, carefully. Even the slightest weakness could cost a hunter his life. The hunting floats, which could keep even the fattest walrus afloat behind the kayak— were they completely watertight? And the summer clothes? Here only the most pleasant work was left to do, to create the beautiful patterns of hair-fine leather strips in red and white.

Osuqo, her mother, and her older sisters worked on her father's and eldest brother's hunting gear and kayaks.

Her father's kayak suit lay in her lap. The thin, almost transparent skin from the intestines of a seal gleamed in the sunshine.

Her head was bent over her work while her fingers

inspected the surface of the kayak. They felt the
warmth from the taut skin. Followed the faintly curved
edge along the kayak's slender top. It ended in a sharp
triangle—almost like the point of a harpoon . . .

The edge of the kayak reminded her of the bone in
a bird's wing.

She was proud of her father's kayak.

Because she had helped to sew it. Because it was
as pretty as a bird, the bird of the sea. Always ready
to take off and begin the hunt for the heavy sea
creatures.

"Are you dreaming? Dreams are for the night and
the winter, Little Sister. Not for work." The voice of her
eldest sister was sharp.

Her head bent a little farther, ashamed. Her fingers
immediately started working on the suit again, and
found a tiny crack in the fine skin.

She was no longer a child!

Wasn't she going to help row the women's boat on
the walrus hunt?

One of the women.

Soon, soon—it would also be time for the marriage
selection. She had seen it for a long time in Poq's eyes.
His gaze—so intimate that her skin had goosebumps
and she wished she was invisible. As distant as the
mountain plateaus, and she had to make herself
visible.

Yes, the selection was near, and she longed for it.

Poq, a great hunter, with the power to wander with

the spirits. That's what the eldest hunters said. Osuqo knew that they were right. Poq received his power that terrible autumn when his father and all his brothers drowned during the whale hunt. But Poq came home with a beautiful fat seal. Since then he had always caught seal, even when the other hunters came home empty-handed. His mother was never hungry again. Was he to live the strict life of an *angakoq*?* Use all of his powers to interpret dreams and omens, listen to the voices of the past and the future? Give all of his endurance and love to the souls of the animals, for the benefit of the people at the settlement?

She believed this was so, hoped it was. Just as she herself dreamed of learning the magic songs which cured illness or brought the reindeer herds to the hunting grounds. The songs that the great shaman knew, whom Osuqo was named after. One day—one day she would also master the songs, fly freely with them in the secret realms between life and death, in the world of the spirits, the souls, and the gods.

She and Poq. After the selection.

The thought filled her with joy so strong it hurt.

Her hands lay idle on the kayak suit.

Her sister cleared her throat loudly.

*Angakoq. The central person in the religious life of the Inuit people was *angakoq* or the shaman. *Angakoq* had the ability to go into a trance in order to let his soul leave his body and wander to the realm of the Moon Man or the Sea Woman (heaven and the underworld). *Angakoq* was the only one in the society who could master the difficult art of going into an ecstatic state and having experiences that could guide and help people in daily life, in illness and death.

Guiltily, Osuqo seized the bone needle again. Her eyes and her fingers concentrated on yet another almost invisible crack in the waterproof suit.

It was hot in the spring sunshine.

Moist surface heat rose from the wet marsh—already a lush green. But beneath the moss the earth was frozen.

Long, quiet hours with sounds both distant and close. The panting of the dogs and the calm chatter of the women, the great gulls circling over the water with shrill hunting cries, the rumbling of the ice floes losing the battle against the sun and the current.

They carried the women's boats down to the shore.

Osuqo came last. She couldn't get a good grip on the boat. It wasn't so heavy, but so awkwardly long and wide.

Right behind her, Little Brother panted and struggled with the kayak over his head. It wasn't easy to control the slender, slight kayak in the spring wind and at the same time watch out for the treacherous sinkholes between the hummocks of the marsh. She could hear him falling in quite often. It would gurgle for a long time when he pulled his foot out again, as if the sinkhole only reluctantly let go of the small foot.

"Go home, Little Brother!" she said impatiently.

He struggled on, stubborn and silent.

Like a fledgling testing its wings for the first time, she thought, and looked lovingly at the small kayak with the chubby legs beneath it.

"Couldn't you have carried the oars for the women's

boat instead? That would have been useful!" She made her voice extra-stern.

There was only a renewed gurgling in reply.

"You can't come with us on the walrus hunt, you know that, don't you? You're too little." Rather shamefully she heard that her voice sounded like her eldest sister's when she herself was scolded.

A sigh of relief came from Little Brother.

They had reached the edge of the steep slope which led down to the shore. Icy water, earth, and fine sand rushed in brown-colored streams down over the slope. The water made the red patterns glow on the large sun-bleached stone surfaces.

Osuqo hesitated, searching for secure footholds on the steaming stones. Little Brother jumped nimbly from stone to stone in front of her. The light kayak rocked in the wind. Almost eagerly, as if it wanted to fly.

Go ahead and fly, little bird, she thought, suddenly proud of her obstinate brother. Soon you, too, will be one of the sea's beautiful birds. Try your wings now!

He ran the last few meters down to the water's edge. The marsh water gurgled in his boots. Osuqo felt a pang of guilt.

I can hear there are big holes in his boots. And they're probably much too small, too. He should have had new ones!

She had started on them, cut out the soles and the shafts of the boots. While the winter storms howled outside the longhouse and the families were gathered in the radiant light and heat of the lamps, she had worked on the boots for Little Brother. But the work had gone slowly, for she would lose herself in the shaman's songs about the joys of life and the sorrows people brought on themselves when they broke the laws and harmed the souls of the animals.

Evening after evening her fingers had played restlessly with the sharp, half-moon-shaped blade of her *ulo*—the women's knife—while her thoughts followed Poq somewhere out on the ice near the seals' breathing hole.

The selection will be in the spring. Then I will receive many tattoos so that my births will be good and our children will be many.

Little Brother had poked her and asked whether his boots would be finished soon.

"Soon, in the spring," she had answered. "I promise you new boots when the ice lets go of the sea."

The kayak lay in the water.

Osuqo looked uneasily at her little brother. He hadn't mentioned the boots since then.

It gurgled with every step he took as he carefully assured himself that everything was in place in the kayak before he slid down into the cockpit and fastened the anorak over the high edge around the hole.

The grass in his boots must be ice-cold and soaking wet. She was afraid that even with the warm reindeer skin in the bottom of the kayak he must be able to feel the cold from the sea.

What if he got sick? What a disaster! And all her fault. Why could she never keep a promise. Do what she was asked to do.

Her guilty conscience conjured up sinister images of a feverish Little Brother. The kayak oar lay securely in his hands, as if he had never done anything but paddle. But this was his very first trip alone.

"You'll get the boots when I come home from the hunt, little bird!" she shouted. "The warmest and most beautiful boots you can imagine! I promise!"

He paddled briskly away.

The kayak cut like an arrow through the waves, slipped supply in and out among the ice floes. Abruptly he turned and raced back toward the shore. His gaze was proud and full of laughter.

Yes, you have the power, just like the great hunters, she thought tenderly. Little Brother, you shall have the most beautiful boots I can make.

"Osuqo!" Her mother's voice was edged with impatience. "Don't you see that you're the only one missing at the oars?"

Osuqo hurried to take her place in the boat. Her mother whispered, still angry: "Your father and brothers are good hunters. You shame them with your dawdling and daydreaming!"

Osuqo didn't answer. Just gripped the oar and fell in with the rowing rhythm of the other women.

Her father, her brothers, and Poq were among the first kayak hunters who paddled swiftly toward the great headland. The kayaks—narrow and low, almost invisible against the dark surface of the water. The strong bodies and arms of the hunters were visible, as was the hunting float behind each man, sharply outlined against the white ice masses. Fragile, vulnerable human bodies, protected only by the skin of the seal and the whale's rib-bone from the ice floes, worn sharp as knives by the spring wind and sun. The kayak hunters were the brave pathfinders in an eternally unknown territory. They had to search out safe passages for the wide women's boats.

Osuqo grew suddenly anxious. She ran her fingers along the cross-seat of the boat. Yes, it was all there: needles, blubber, sinew, and the scraps of skin, everything that was necessary to save a hunter's life if his kayak were damaged.

The kayaks had reached the headland.

Behind them lay a channel of open water.

The women's boats followed.

Osuqo saw her father's kayak round the headland. She heard him shout before he disappeared.

"They've spotted walrus!" her mother yelled happily. "Row faster!"

As soon as they rounded the headland, Osuqo saw it. Her hands grew cold with fear.

It was enormous—many times bigger than a women's boat. The ship was black, heavy, threatening. It glided slowly toward them. The great sails had the color of old ice. They snapped sharply in the wind. The huge bow crushed the ice masses with a high-pitched, plaintive sound.

Here it was, the sinister black bird from her nightmares.

Osuqo recognized it all too well—the heavy black body, the mighty, dirty gray wings that slowly folded as the bird made itself ready. Ready for *what* she did not know. The nightmares always ended here, as the bird turned toward her.

"Sit still, Osuqo!" Her mother's voice was stern. "You've seen the foreigners' ships many times before. Why are you worried now?"

Of course, but always from a safe distance up at the longhouses. From there they were as small as toy boats, and they would disappear if she just closed her eyes long enough. But now it was different.

Her hands ached, convulsively clutching the oar.

She pulled it in and dried her hands on her sealskin pants. The fur felt warm and comforting and she grew calm again.

She must not behave like a child. She knew that the foreigners only came to trade.

Her father had often traded seal and reindeer skins, walrus and narwhal tusks or blubber for beautiful beads, bits of iron, and colorful, soft cloth.

The dark ship lay silent, waiting.

The kayaks had almost reached it.

The men waved the women's boats to follow.

Osuqo rowed with the same brisk rhythm as the other women. They talked excitedly about everything they wished for this time: cooking pots of clay, needles of iron, and many, many beads.

Osuqo rowed silently with bowed head. She did not look up until the women's boat thudded against the side of the ship. It loomed above her like a steep black mountain. Then she saw the foreigners for the first time in her life.

They were standing at the railing, high overhead.

[15

Pale faces shone against the blue sky. Around the faces was a profusion of hair and beards in as many colors as the mountains had before the snow came. Even their hands were hairy.

Osuqo shuddered. She had never seen anything so hideous.

Their voices sounded like the barking of angry dogs, at times high and piercing, at times far back in their throats, as if they were growling.

The women in the women's boats took out skins and blubber and pieces of bone that they could use to trade for the glittering beads. The most eager among them took off their sealskin knee boots, or *kamiks*, and their outer furs.

In the meantime, the men had started shouting up to the foreigners in a language that Osuqo vaguely recognized as her own.

Two of the women's boats were sent back to the settlement for more skins, walrus tusks, and blubber.

Don't do it, she wanted to say. Let's just trade what we have and get away. Fast!

But she knew that they wouldn't listen to her.

They didn't listen to the old shaman either when he warned them against having too much to do with the foreigners. Why should they listen to her—Osuqo, almost grownup—who did not yet have enough power to interpret her own dreams?

Suddenly she could smell the foreign ship. Suffocating and heavy. It made her nauseated and even more afraid.

She had to think about something else.

Her fingers cautiously touched the side of the ship. Rough and hard as the driftwood that the spring storms tossed up on the shore near the settlement, the precious wood that became beams in the longhouses, the shafts of harpoons, and powerful, fine amulets. She yearned for the safety of the longhouses and for Little Brother, who was waiting for them.

Her father's kayak lay beside the women's boat.

He was talking to her: "Do you hear me? Come on. The foreigners want us to visit the ship."

She stared at him, uncomprehending.

"Come on, Osuqo," he repeated urgently. "The foreigners have invited us . . . We must show them respect and courtesy. They have only invited *you* and *me* to come aboard.

"And Poq," he added quickly, when he saw that she still hesitated.

She had to obey, that was clear. And if Poq dared, she had to as well.

Her mother smiled proudly at her. She looked in confusion from her father to the looming side of the ship. But how . . .

"Just follow me," said her father.

Along the side of the ship hung two ladders made of thick rope. Poq was already climbing up one of them, and her father climbed up the other. Osuqo followed, slowly.

Her heart was pounding loudly in her breast.

Now she was close to the end of the nightmare. Soon she would find out what the black bird wanted.

[17

* * *

The deck of the ship was enormous. Dark and slippery as ice.

Osuqo stared as if spellbound at the foreigners. There were many of them, and they were big. They were standing in a tight semicircle around Poq and her father.

The man in the middle of the semicircle was taller than the others. His hands were large and covered with thick red hair. The same color as his beard and his curly hair. He was the one doing most of the talking. His voice was forceful, deep, and almost growling.

He smiled often, but the smile vanished just as quickly as the spring clouds before the sun.

Her father spoke mostly to the red-haired man. Almost deferentially, Osuqo heard. With words that sounded foreign to her ears, he bade them welcome to the fjord with the great icebergs. He told them with pride that Poq was a great hunter who would soon become his son, and that she—Osuqo—was his youngest daughter.

The men turned toward her. She met the eyes of the red-haired man. His gaze was pale blue, cold, and infinitely deep. She was staring right into her nightmare. The black bird turned toward her and opened its powerful, sharp beak.

His gaze paralyzed her. She felt the railing press into her back, but she couldn't move, could not utter a sound or close her eyes. He was the one who shifted his gaze and broke the bond between them. He smiled quickly, at once triumphant and threatening. He knew what she had seen in his eyes, but what did that matter? She was helpless and alone.

Her father and Poq were in the midst of trading. They ran back and forth to the railing to get new armfuls of dried fish, whale meat, blubber, and fine walrus tusks. They placed everything in piles at the feet of the foreigners, stepped back respectfully, and waited.

The foreigners whispered to each other, kicked the blubber, and felt the skins and the walrus tusks. They didn't seem very interested, thought Osuqo, growing indignant on her father's behalf. He had used many words to tell them how fine the skins were.

The red-haired man stood motionless. He was leaning on a strange stick that vaguely resembled a powerful spear but without the spearhead.

All at once he began talking to her father. For a long time.

But her father didn't understand.

"What does he want?" he wondered aloud.

Poq's face revealed nothing. "Don't know," he said curtly. "Let's trade what we have and get away from here."

The red-haired man grabbed her father's shoulder, pulled him closer, and talked loud, right into his face. Impatiently he pointed toward the walrus tusks and sketched something in the air.

Her father winced. He looked with embarrassment

at Poq, but he didn't understand what the foreigner meant either.

The other foreigners joined in. Talking excitedly, louder. One of them drew a picture on the deck of a peculiar animal, almost like a reindeer. It didn't have the reindeer's large antlers but a long, thin horn in the middle of its forehead. The foreigner pointed from the drawing to the walrus tusks, over and over again.

Poq and her father looked at each other.

"An animal like that doesn't exist," her father said firmly.

"But . . . it's not the animal they mean," replied Poq slowly. "Just the horn. Don't you see what it looks like? The narwhal's horn. Those scraps of horn we have left from the hunt last year, aren't they lying in the women's boats? Give them horns, if that's what they want. Then we can get away from here! These foreigners mean misfortune for us, I'm sure of that."

Osuqo had never heard Poq speak so seriously and adamantly.

So he knew it, too.

But her father didn't pay any attention to him. He was much too absorbed in being friendly, giving the foreigners what they wanted for their precious bits of iron, beads, and pieces of cloth.

Politely he asked the red-haired man to wait while the women took out the two finest polar-bear skins and the pieces of narwhal horn. When they reached the deck, he carried them proudly over to the red-haired man.

This ought to have pacified the foreigners so the

trade could finally be concluded. The men crowded around the eight arm-length pieces of horn. Grabbed them greedily and weighed them in their hands. They nodded, smiling, at the polar-bear skins.

But the red-haired man was not pleased. He yelled something at Father, loud and impatient. His hands sketched eagerly in the air.

"More! More!" translated Osuqo. "Father, the foreigners are greedy, they only want more! But we don't have any more pieces of narwhal horn. Let's do as Poq says, Father. Let's . . ."

Her father didn't listen. He was offended and hurt. How could the foreigners be so ungrateful? Didn't they realize that this was all they had left after the poor winter hunt? With great dignity he spoke:

The terrible storm had raged for many days and nights and had forced the hunters to shore. The storm had come after a long autumn with poor hunting. In the longhouses many were sick and still more were hungry. Something was wrong. Something had made the Sea Woman so furious and offended that she was keeping the whales away from the people's hunting grounds. The old shaman, Aua, nodded gravely and said that the laws had been broken. There was only one way out. He must journey down to the Sea Woman and calm her.

Aua's soul left his body and set out on the dangerous journey to the home of the goddess at the bottom of the sea.

The goddess was furious and despondent, and her

beautiful hair was tangled from the people's sins.

The shaman was horrified. Who had wounded the souls of the sea creatures so deeply? He didn't know, but he was filled with remorse and sympathy. He picked out the lice, carefully combed out the tangles in her long hair, while he praised the souls of the animals with beautiful songs. At last the Sea Woman grew happy again, and she promised to send the sea animals back to the people's hunting grounds.

While his soul wandered, Aua's body lay like an empty shell. The people in the longhouse kept an anxious vigil over it one day and one night. Then his soul returned, but so exhausted that yet another day passed while the soul rested in the motionless body.

It was not until the third day that Aua awakened. Then the storm abated. The hunters could go out again, but they returned disappointed.

The Sea Woman had sent only one narwhal. That could only mean that the people's sins were more serious than Aua had realized. After that, it took a long time for the hunting to be good again, but by then the narwhals had wandered on.

While Father spoke, the foreigners were talking loudly to each other in their own language. They were not in the least interested in his explanation. They were just greedy for more horns.

Why? Osuqo couldn't understand it. The foreigners had gotten the finest skins, the best of everything that the people at the settlement could spare. Wasn't that enough?

The foreigners were talking louder, more impatiently among themselves. The red-haired man grabbed her father's arm and pulled him over to the railing. He talked even louder, friendly, persuasive, while he pointed at the kayaks by the side of the ship. Her father shook his head decisively. His face was stiff with indignation.

"What do they want, Father?" Osuqo heard the panic quavering in her voice. She felt disaster approaching, as swiftly as storm clouds gather in the sky.

"They want our kayaks," her father answered shortly. "But this is enough. They have gotten all that we have to give." He crossed his arms. His gaze was dignified, defiant.

The red-haired man made new signs, excitedly: "Not *trade*, just *look at!*" The quick smile flickered across his face.

"Let them have their way!" Poq's voice was sharp. "Let's get this over with, so we can leave!"

Her father hesitated, but Poq did not wait for his permission. He asked her eldest brother to send up his own and her father's kayaks.

Why couldn't the foreigners climb *down* to look at the kayaks? thought Osuqo fearfully. She pressed herself harder against the railing and looked at the kayaks. Like two wet, wounded sea birds, they lay on the vast deck. Beautiful, lifeless under the foreigners' hands, which scratched and clawed, tore off the hunting lines and the hunting floats, tried the spears and the harpoons. All the while talking loud and laughing.

The red-haired man was eager, smiling. But his cold

gaze flickered from Poq to her father to her and back to the kayaks.

Then she realized that they would never get the kayaks back. She also knew that the black bird was going to attack.

Osuqo never had time to warn her father. Suddenly an arm lay in an iron grip around her waist, squeezing the breath out of her. A coarse piece of cloth was stuffed into her mouth.

Osuqo was terrified.

She threw back her head.

She heard the sound of bones being crushed and a roar of pain.

She was thrown down brutally.

Hard fists and heavy boots pressed her face and body against the filthy deck. Her arms were tied behind her back with a thick rope.

Osuqo forced her head up, in time to see a club strike the back of Poq's head, sending him bleeding to the deck. Four foreigners tied his arms and legs and slung him aside like a bundle of skins.

Osuqo saw her father.

Three foreigners threw themselves at him. Hammered away with clenched fists at his head and body. They struggled to bring him to his knees. He fought them, furious and wounded.

Osuqo had never seen her father like this.

Her father, calm, gentle, and compliant, had acquired the strength and courage of a polar bear. The foreigners couldn't break him. Never, never.

Pride and rage filled Osuqo and gave her new strength.

She cast her head from side to side, spit, heaved until her mouth was free of the disgusting piece of cloth and she could shriek her outrage.

A hairy hand immediately clamped down over her mouth and stopped all sound.

Her face was pressed against the deck again. The pain in her neck, nose, and mouth extinguished her rage, but could not keep out the cries of distress from the women's boats and the kayaks. Her mother, who begged the foreigners to release her family. Her eldest brother, who furiously demanded that the rope ladders be put down again so that he and the other hunters could come up and negotiate, give them anything in return for the freedom of his father, his sister, and his friend.

The foreigners ignored them.

Suddenly Osuqo realized why. The assault had been planned all along. The black bird had just been waiting for the chance to attack. Now she faced its evil will, but she would never, never bow to it!

The knowledge gave her new strength. She struggled to get free, but the iron grip around her mouth tightened and the sharp boot edges cut deeper into her back and thighs.

Osuqo defied the pain, forced her head up and saw her father. He was standing alone, had thrown off his attackers as if they were squealing puppies. His face was contorted with pain, but his eyes smoldered with pride.

Osuqo knew that she would never forget that look—stronger than death.

Everything happened terribly fast then.

Her father at one moment loomed alone over his whimpering attackers. In the next moment he began a furious assault on the strangers who were holding Osuqo pinned to the deck.

Then she saw the red-haired man suddenly right behind her father. Calmly, almost indifferently, he lifted the strange spear and aimed it at her father's head. She had to warn him!

Had to get her mouth free!

The hairy iron hand had her mouth clamped shut. She bit it, hard. Felt warm blood fill her mouth and the grip loosen.

"*Father!*" she howled.

But her shout and the foreigner's roar of pain were drowned in a deafening bang, louder than the crash of an iceberg caving in.

Her father was standing right over her.

There was a powerful shudder in his body, as if he had received a violent blow. His knees buckled, trembling.

Osuqo was terrified. Her father was wounded! How? The red-haired man had not stabbed or struck with the spear. What had happened?

The red-haired man lowered the spear. Waited. The cold eyes followed her father, who slowly fell to his knees.

Osuqo stared straight into her father's wide-open,

astonished eyes. He opened his mouth, wanted to say something.

But no words came out, only blood. It poured out of his mouth, thick, warm, and red. Flowed down over the kayak suit. Ran in small rivulets toward Osuqo.

His hand clenched, opened powerlessly.

Unsteadily he moved it toward his mouth, wanted to stop the blood, say something. But he fell forward. The other hand stretched out, as if to protect her. It remained there, motionless, next to her cheek. The palm turned upward.

The iron grip around her mouth was gone.

She put her face in her father's open hand and howled as long as she could.

Beyond her own grief, she heard the furious voice of her eldest brother, the growls and roars of the foreigners. The sounds of a struggle for life and death, her brother alone against the attackers. She heard a new, horrible bang, her brother's gasp of pain, the body dragged across the deck.

Beyond her own pain, she heard the body fall into the water, the chorus of wailing and weeping from the women's boats.

Beyond everything that was familiar tramped foreign feet, resounded unfamiliar barks of command.

There was a deep, restless rumble inside the ship. The fearsome black bird was in the process of taking off. It was going to take her along. Where?

What awaited her beyond the familiar? Nothing other than terror. Nothing. Nothing . . .

No! It thundered inside her head, but her voice didn't have the strength to bring it forth. Her mouth was silent in her father's motionless hand.

It was colder now.

The tears felt warm against her cool skin.

The ship moved slowly. Creaked and sighed.

The wailing from the women's boats grew fainter and fainter.

Boots approached and stopped.

She didn't have the strength to raise her eyes.

Her head thudded against the deck when her father's body was taken from her. Grief cut like a knife when his body hit the waves.

Proud, worthy Father,
you who are a great hunter.
Your soul shall wander with the souls of the sea animals.
Play happily with them,
sing beautifully about the mysteries of life and death.
Receive your eldest son with love,
meet his arrogance with tenderness.
Speak well of my mother and my sisters and brothers to
the Sea Woman
so they will always have enough to eat.
Don't ever forsake me in the unknown,
as I will never forsake you, thought Osuqo.

She was so terribly tired. But she followed her father's journey to the bottom of the sea with all her strength and love.

A chubby little boy with gurgling boots and a rocking kayak on his head still forced his way into her thoughts.

He would never get his beautiful, warm boots.

Her mother would never have the grandchildren she wished for.

Poq would never come for her in the longhouse.

The black bird had torn everything apart.

The first day in Osuqo's adult life had become the day her life ended.

"*O*nly one summer," Father had said. "I'll be away from you only one summer."

Mother and I looked away when he said that. We had heard it so many times before. It was never just one summer.

He said it anyway, every spring before the heavy whaling ship sailed north to Spitsbergen and the storms there. The summer always turned to fall before the ship returned, weather-beaten, with my sick and exhausted father. Every time, he swore that it was his last trip. But just as surely as the spring rains came, he would sign on again.

"God help me, it's all I know how to do"—and he sighed each time.

"Only one summer," he had said. Yet everything was different.

For the ship he had signed on was foreign, and the destination of the journey was unknown.

The rumors buzzed around the marketplaces and along the wharves.

Brownish-black and gloomy, the heavy Dutch ship

lay ready to sail at Vågen. The English captain who was to command the ship for the rich merchants in town was a hard man and an adventurer, it was said. Just the kind of man who could defy the dangers of that mysterious land.

"Meta Incognita" was the name of the land, some said. When the ships neared the coast, they were swallowed up by thick fog which forced them to sail around helplessly. Week after week, blinded by the dense whiteness, deafened by the oppressive silence, the ships sailed until they sank. But the souls of the dead found no rest. They had to roam forever in the white darkness.

"Greenland" was what other people thought the land was called. Not green at all, as the name implied, but ice-cold white. Like a glittering diamond, it lured ships to its shores. Then the storms broke loose, and deranged sea monsters flung themselves upon the helpless ships and drove them into whirling masses of ice. There the sailors died, while the storms raged and the evil monsters howled with laughter.

"The land of our ancestors," others claimed. The land the Norwegians had discovered many hundreds of years ago, which was wonderfully fertile, which had hot springs and lush grass, greener than any other place in the world. Our forefathers settled in this green country, but the icebergs towered up along the shores and formed impenetrable walls. Our forefathers were unable to leave their paradise, or to flee from the wild savages who ravaged and burned and killed people and livestock.

Confused and afraid, I listened to the stories buzzing around the marketplace. I hoped that it was just lies and fabrication.

That's all I could do, because Father didn't listen to our pleas to stay home.

I tried again the last night.

The spring rain drummed against our house at a slant.

Inside my head, it was drumming just as hard. Probably because I had cried so much that day.

I lay in Father's arms. His heart beat calmly. His homespun jacket had a safe smell of tobacco and his warm body. One hand lay softly around my neck. The other was gently stroking my bad arm.

It hurt like fire. Maybe it was because of the spring rain. Maybe because Father was going away.

My pleas were useless.

"The sea is my life, Christine," he said softly. "I have no choice. It is God's will and the King's command that the best sailors in the country have to find that godforsaken land with the unfortunate descendants of our forefathers. We're also supposed to find the unknown Northwest Passage to India and Cathay. I am one of those chosen—can I refuse to go?"

I didn't answer.

Mother's head was bent over her sewing.

Her hands, working calmly on Father's shirt, were trembling slightly. Even in the dying light from the hearth I could see it.

Mother never cried, but her anxiety drew hard lines around her mouth and made her hands quiver like an old woman's. She would be like that until Father came home.

"After all, I'm going for Mother and you, Christine." His voice was imploring. "I only have you, and you only have me. After this trip, we'll never have to worry about the future, because . . ."

He stopped there at the painful part, but I knew the rest of it all too well: ". . . you can't get married, Christine, not without a proper dowry." Otherwise, what man would take a poor sailor's daughter with a crippled arm, ugly as the work of the devil?

Meta Incognita.

The journey to the unknown, to infinity, to the utmost boundary of the world. Beyond Meta Incognita, a great sorrow was, perhaps, waiting for Mother and me.

Father felt me trembling.

"I'm going to trust you with a secret," he whispered, right up close to my ear. "Promise me, dear child— not a word to anyone?"

I nodded.

"Captain Davis has taken me into his confidence. His real mission for the King of England is to find"— Father lowered his voice—"the land of the unicorns! People have searched for the land of the unicorns for centuries without finding it. No one has ever caught those shy, beautiful animals who only let themselves be tamed by young maidens, but many have found the unicorn's horn. Captain Davis has found many unicorn horns in the green land. This time he wants to capture the animals and bring them back. We, who know the secret, will get our generous share. Think what that will mean for us . . ."

He didn't have to say any more. I thought—and dreamed.

I had seen the precious unicorn horns myself once at the pharmacist's. Just a little piece, of course, before it was crushed to a fine yellowish-white powder and sold to the richest old men in town, the ones who were courting young maidens.

"When we find the land of the unicorn, our fortune will be made," Father continued elatedly. "For a horn is worth six times its weight in gold, and you shall have the most beautiful horn I can find. Maybe I'll even catch a young animal, which you, my fair maiden, can tame."

The dream about the unicorn held at bay the fear of crushing ice floes and howling sea monsters that summer.

I dreamed about it every night, and soon the dream became more real than the days, with their heavy toil and waiting.

It was small and slender, no larger than a foal. Its coat was shiny and a soft grayish-white, its hooves were small and the color of mother-of-pearl. The beautiful horn was pale rose. Almost transparent when the unicorn shook its head and the sunbeams caught the horn in their white light. It stared at me with black eyes. Its gaze was solemn and searching.

All at once it grew rigid, as if sensing danger. In the next instant it vanished, melting into the deep shadows under the trees.

Just as suddenly it was there again, motionless in the middle of a patch of sunlight. Its coat was covered by a pattern of dancing shadows from the crowns of the trees. Its gaze was mysterious and enticing. It wanted to show me something, but I never had a chance to find out what it was.

I always woke up, warm with longing to follow it, full of shame because I wanted to catch it.

The unicorn was my consolation—my secret alone. Mother had only the fear.

Mother had always been quiet. This summer it was as if she was locked in a room, and I felt guilty. But I couldn't tell her about the unicorn.

The silence grew between us. We talked little to each other, and never about Father.

Long before daybreak, we got up, said our prayers, and walked in silence to Master Mowinckel's house.

Mother walked in front, stiff and proud. I followed behind, dizzy from the night's dreams and the prickling pains in my arm.

In the sleeping house we quickly started in on the day's work.

We lit a fire in the hearth, fetched water, emptied

the garbage, made breakfast for the master and mistress, the hired hands, and the clerks, washed dishes, washed the floors, washed clothes, went to the market, cooked, patched, darned. Dragged, carried, scrubbed, without a break until matins. Then we were free to go home, still silent. Mother in front, just as proud as in the morning, but with a more rounded back. Me behind, staggering from exhaustion and pain, and with only one thought in my head—to stretch my aching body on the bed and surrender myself to the dreams.

As the summer slowly disappeared in hard workdays and restless nights, the little unicorn was with me more and more. In the midst of fish guts and stinking bed straw it would suddenly be standing there, with that pale rose horn glittering in the sunshine. While Madame Mowinckel's curses rained down on me, I would suddenly meet that enticing gaze. It was as though it was protecting me, even against Master Mowinckel's more and more frequent outbreaks of rage.

Mother had no consolation. She suffered the most during the master's terrible moods. As if it was Mother's and my fault that the ship hadn't returned yet.

"Only one summer," Father had said.

Now the summer had passed into autumn storms with icy rain, without any news of the Dutch ship.

The rumors about what had happened buzzed like bees in a honeypot. The ship had been crushed by ice floes, swallowed by sea monsters, overrun by wild savages. There was no end to the gruesome prophecies of death and destruction.

The stories flew in the hired hands' quarters, in the

master's parlor, and in the marketplaces, but silence always fell whenever Mother or I arrived. Deafeningly quiet, as though we had gone deaf. Mouths were buttoned up and eyes averted.

They had given up hope. Condemned Father and the others to perdition.

They didn't scare me, because I had my unicorn.

As long as it was there, in my dreams, in my toil and in my hope, I was safe. Let them gossip on in their prophecies, and we'd show them when Father got home!

Besides, I understood the art of waiting.

I'd had to learn it early.

"Just one summer" meant that your heart could beat calmly until the first month of autumn was past. Then the waiting began, all the quick visits to the wharves, listening to the people gossiping, and your heart would beat uneasily. I could hold out this way for one more month.

After that, the waiting was intolerable. Nothing could stop the frightening thoughts about what might have happened. I learned to command my body to scrub and wash as though nothing had happened, but I couldn't keep it from suddenly shaking as in a fever when my heart said that the waiting was in vain.

The violent storms gave way to frozen silence. Winter was approaching. Still no sign of the Dutch ship.

Mother found strength in prayer. Envious, I watched her clasped hands and her lips moving soundlessly through the long, sleepless nights. My strength had left me.

The little unicorn had faded beneath the trees. It moved like a shadow in a mirror, flickering and distant. I tried to reach it, but a crushed ship in thundering ice floes forced it away, and me into exhausting fear.

Inside me, chaos ruled; outside, everything was still.

I no longer saw the town, the people, the weather. Only heavy seas and struggling bodies. I no longer heard voices. Only the crash of the sea drowning out the cries for help.

Once in a great while something would penetrate the chaos. Words that jabbed like sharp needles, but which I had to listen to.

It was the quiet conversation between Master Mowinckel and the other merchants who had put their money into the Dutch ship. More and more often they would gather in the semidarkness of the master's parlor, smoking and talking, talking and smoking in the late afternoon. More restlessly, more heatedly with each day that passed with no news.

They were afraid for different reasons than I was, the town's richest men.

They talked about who was going to make up their losses, who would have to bear the responsibility. Their accusations were directed against the master, I noticed. *He* was the one who had chosen the English captain; *he* was the one who had begged the King for permission to sail to Greenland; and *he* was the one who had convinced them to invest their money in the ill-fated ship. The highborn merchants whined as though the end of the world was at hand, but they had not one word for the sailors or their poor families.

"Father! Father!" I called silently when their yammering about money became too painful. In this way I suppressed my fear with rage for a while, long enough to catch my breath before I sank into the depths of sorrow again.

"All hope is lost. They're never coming back."

It blew like a wind through the town, from the fishing boats along the wharves to the water pumps in the marketplace.

The waiting was over.

In the half-light of Master Mowinckel's parlor the accusations and whining fell silent. Now there was tense, solemn talk of how the loss was to be divided. Still not a word about the sailors, about my father who was lost forever.

The chaos within me had subsided. I floated motionless at the bottom, unable to protect myself from the memories of Father, who lifted me laughing in his arms, Father's worried face above my aching arm, Father's ice-blue flashing eyes which cut into the little boys who teased me, Father's urgent voice whispering the secret of the unicorn.

Among the memories, a little unicorn with black eyes which no longer saw me.

Life continued, as though there had never been any ship or any dream of discovering the unknown route to India and Cathay, and huge riches in the icy desolation.

People no longer spoke to Mother and me. It was as though we had become invisible, along with our sorrow.

The merchants met less and less often in the twilight at Master Mowinckel's. Even they no longer mentioned the ship. They talked calmly about next year's whaling at Spitsbergen.

It would soon be Christmas. People had busy days ahead.

Only we who had lost fathers or sons aboard the Dutch ship had something else to think about: Were the gruesome stories true? Did the souls of sailors have to wander forever? How would the families manage without the men to provide for them?

In spite of everything, Mother and I were lucky.

Master Mowinckel offered us both permanent work, and lodging in the bed-closet in the kitchen. The master never mentioned Father, but I knew that it was his good name that brought us security. We accepted it gratefully.

Our little house was freezing in the wintertime. Only Father had kept the hearth burning and the cold out.

Mother and I had neither time nor energy for it now. Every time I opened the door at home, the longing for Father struck me like an ice-cold breaker.

We were two frozen servant souls who fled to the kitchen warmth of the master's house. But we did our best to be invisible, for the coldness that Madame Mowinckel directed at us was deadly.

While the master scarcely noticed that we were in the house, Madame Mowinckel noticed us all the more. Her entire black-clad figure, stiffer now than before Mother and I moved in, made that clear.

Everything about her frightened me.

Her thin hands, like pale bird claws. Her narrow face above the tight black collar. Colorless except for her thin mouth, red like congealed blood. Only when her eyes met mine did her face get some color. Then two deep red spots would bloom on her cheeks like rare roses. But they were not beautiful. I was sure that it was fear and hatred that lent color to her cheeks. Maybe she was afraid of our grief like some contagious disease. Maybe she hated me and my crippled arm, like the work of the devil. For Madame Mowinckel was quite God-fearing.

She watched over Mother and me like a prison guard who has been given custody of two mortally dangerous convicts. I couldn't always see her black-clad figure, but I could see the sharp shadow, smell her nauseating powder, or hear her silk dress rustle angrily.

Madame Mowinckel filled the house with an intense feeling of suspicion and pent-up rage.

She plagued me the way the vapor of brimstone pricks at your nose. Her malevolent feelings turned against Mother and me, but I could feel that her bitter hatred was older than our misfortune.

The time before Christmas gave us more work than ever.

There was no end to it. We toiled from daybreak until far into the night, always with Madame Mowinckel's rage at the back of our necks. Only when she went to bed did her shadows vanish, and the rooms in the house became normal again. Filled with peace and the creaking of woodwork, the smell of tar and fish entrails, and the sleeping sounds from the hired hands' quarters and the bed-closets of the family.

The late-night hours were our best time, almost too good to sleep away. The hearth was allowed to burn all night now that Mother and I were watching it. It helped keep the other rooms warm during those biting-cold days before Christmas, and it helped warm the beds of Master and Madame, their daughter Sofie, and their son Henrik.

The first nights after we moved in, I had lain quite still in the cramped, dark bed-closet, letting the grief and pain tear at me as they would. My arm burned like fire, my heart ached. The thought of Father stung like an open wound. In the daytime the drudgery kept everything at a distance, but when the silence and I were alone in the bed-closet, nothing could stop my despair.

Caught in a net of painful questions: Why did it have to be Father? How did he die? Where was he now? What had we done to be punished so severely?

I couldn't stand the loneliness in the dark. It was better to sit with Mother on the edge of the hearth, near her prayers, even though I couldn't join in with them.

God didn't hear me. He had never heard my prayers. As far back as I could remember, I had begged forgiveness for the sins that had made me crippled, for scandalous thoughts and deeds left undone.

But no matter how long I knelt by the bed, or on

the cold stone floor in church, no matter how hard I clasped my hands and closed my eyes, the prayers felt like pebbles in my mouth and dry leaves in my heart.

God didn't listen to me because His wrath was greater than His mercy, I was sure of that.

But I couldn't tell Mother that—she who deadened her grief with prayer.

I was at peace next to Mother and the glowing embers in the night.

Only rarely was my peace disturbed.

The door creaked. Henrik sneaked in.

With a friendly, apologetic look at Mother and me, he sat down quietly on the edge of the hearth. He could sit there for a long time in silence, staring into the coals, before he would get up, nod, and disappear just as soundlessly as he had come.

What was Henrik thinking?

All I knew was that he was completely unlike the rest of the family. Henrik was barely seventeen, tall and thin, with hands that were much too big. They were always red, as if it was there his blushing was most apparent.

He was wise and clever, soon on his way to the King's Copenhagen to study medicine and theology. That was Madame Mowinckel's great pride. But the tight, threadbare clothes and his eternal stammering and blushing were a source of her rage.

"How is he supposed to get along among the worldly

Copenhageners?" she would complain loudly to everyone who came to visit.

I hoped that the worldly Copenhageners would see the good person underneath the stammering and the clumsy movements.

He had sat in the kitchen for many nights before he opened his mouth.

"All hope is not lost, believe me!"

Only one stuttering sentence. As soon as the words had been forced out, he blushed intensely, got up, and stumbled toward the door.

Mother was imperturbable in her prayers.

I stared openmouthed at the door for a long time. "All hope is not lost." What did he mean? What did he know about the Dutch ship?

It bothered me for many days, but I found no answer. For Henrik didn't come at night after that, and he avoided me during the day. I sought him out, begged him with my eyes: "Tell me what you know!" But he was as silent as a closed room.

Still, I felt better for a while. Both because Henrik had given me back a hope I no longer had, and because he cared about how Mother and I felt. In the Mowinckel house, sympathy was a rarity.

Sofie was the direct opposite of her brother Henrik. She was barely a year younger. Plump, people said, but I thought she was fat. A big pink body that bulged inside tight silk casings. Always dressed as if she were on her way to a party.

Madame Mowinckel worshiped her daughter and bragged uninhibitedly about her beauty—that pink pouting mouth, those pale blue eyes, those flaxen curls. That voice, sweet as honey.

But Madame Mowinckel never heard her when her voice was transformed to whiplashes: when the pillows weren't fluffed enough, or fresh flowers were missing by her bed. Then Miss Sofie would tell me whose child I was, and what God had intended for the likes of me. Gone was the pink honey-sweet beauty that infatuated men young and old. What was left was an ill-tempered young girl, with a tongue as poisonous as an adder's.

Only the servants, Henrik, and I got to see the other side of Madame Mowinckel's favorite. How I hated and envied her! She had everything I lacked, and she knew how to torture me with it.

She never turned her maliciousness loose on Mother. There was something that curbed Miss Sofie's wrath. Maybe she also saw Mother as an unapproachable queen in a secret realm far from our world.

Christmas came, and went.

For Mother and me, Christmas was nothing but more work. Long days with the smell of frying food, steaming drinks, laughter and loud voices, rustling silk, winter-wet homespun, and new leather.

Master Mowinckel was a God-fearing man who celebrated Christmas both at home and in church, but he never let a chance go by to offer food and drink. Never had there been the occasion for so many festivities as during this Christmas season, for the unmarried men of the town poured in to court the marriageable Miss Sofie. There were pale youths hanging on the skirts of strict mothers, and worldly dandies, solid ship's captains, and blustering merchants, and the powerful Dr. Abraham.

He came often, that old pig. Sat in the parlor, so heavy and fat that his thighs bulged over the bench and his paunch threatened to burst his expensive silk vest. Jabbered away in French and Latin with that thin, piercing voice, while he swallowed Miss Sofie with his tiny red-rimmed eyes.

He came as often as decency would permit. Madame Mowinckel enjoyed his unabashed admiration for her daughter, and the master's broad face beamed with pride at the fact that the rich, learned doctor—who had been a widower for a dozen years—now honored him, the master, by courting the young Miss Sofie.

She basked in all this attention. Round and pink in wheat-colored silk, she sat between her parents, with her eyes shyly downcast and a triumphant little smile on that pouting red mouth.

I rushed in and out with steaming mulled wine, strong ale, and sweets. It made my flesh crawl when I saw the doctor, like a fat black bird, devour her with his eyes.

Don't have anything to do with him! I wanted to whisper. Wait! Choose someone else. He will be your downfall!

But I didn't dare. What good would it have done if I, the crippled servant girl, had given advice to the beautiful daughter of the merchant? She would probably have taken it as an insult and gotten her father to throw me out for my impudence and envy.

God knows I was envious of her, but I didn't envy her that! I didn't envy her the fate that awaited her, either.

Dr. Abraham came more and more often, and the other suitors came more seldom.

The conversations between the doctor and the master became more serious. About money, property, and dowry. The master was eager to make a good bargain. It was no wonder; he had lost a lot of money on the Dutch ship.

The doctor was at the bursting point from impatience and desire. Together they wove the net of engagement party and wedding plans and trading in goods and gold which would hold Miss Sofie captive forever. She sat between them the whole time, with her sweet smile. I knew that her thoughts were elsewhere, in colorful dreams of banquets, silk, and jewels. Didn't she understand anything?

I began to feel sorry for her. The need to warn her grew stronger as the net tightened around the dreaming maiden, barely two months older than I was. I had to get out of the parlor fast, before I said something I would regret.

In the cool darkness between the parlor and the kitchen I was able to collect myself again.

I was standing there one evening, nauseated and furious about the disgusting game the two men were playing with Miss Sofie's life. Then there was a sudden creak in the floor near me. A shadow came right up to me. Henrik's voice whispered low and fast: "Trust me, all hope is not lost! All hope is not lost! Now, soon!"

I gazed around me with eyes wide open, searching with fear in the darkness. My heart was pounding hard. There was no one to be seen. The darkness was soundless, but the blood roared in my ears.

Was it a dream? Or was it really Henrik? I was sure of his voice, but whether he had been *here* or inside my head, I didn't know.

"All hope—all hope—all hope is not lost!"

The words whirled around in my head. What did they mean? All at once the gate of my dreams was flung open again. The silent darkness was filled with Father. Father. Laughing toward me with sun-filled eyes. Frothing masses of water breaking over a helpless body. The unicorn unmoving, with dancing shadows on its soft pelt.

As if frozen, I stood there in the dark.

Sorrow and dreams whirled around. An open wound that had started to heal.

How did I cross the endless darkness to the light and warmth of the kitchen? I don't know. Suddenly I was there, next to Mother, by the hearth where she was calmly stirring a pot.

The tears came unexpectedly, like a torrent in the spring.

She carried me like a little child to the bed-closet. Rocked me gently in her arms.

Sobbing, I cried over and over: "Father! *Father!* It'll never end! Never, never, never . . ."

"I know, child," she murmured, stroking me, drying the tears and mucus on my burning skin. "My child, I know, I know."

I hadn't wept for Father yet, only let the grief sink to the bottom. On top of the grief I had piled hours, days, and weeks. Like stones on top of a grave. A few incomprehensible words had uncovered the longing, just as painful as when the waiting ended.

I cried for a long time.

Mother whispered and rocked me, warming us both. For the first time in a long while together, in desperate love and dreams.

It's only a dream! I thought with clenched teeth.

But it was no dream.

The news came with the fresh spring wind.

The rumors were borne on the ships, grew in the marketplaces, swelled up by the water pumps, and were multiplied in the market stalls.

"The Dutch ship is on its way back! It'll be here at any moment! Loaded full of riches and rarities . . ."

I didn't want to hear any more. Refused to believe that the rumors were true. Was unable to start waiting all over again.

Mother and I had shared our grief after that Christmas night. It was no longer so lonely, so desolate and cold.

We had begun to talk a little about Father.

Cautiously we started to talk about what our future might be.

We could continue working for Master Mowinckel. It wasn't the worst of fates. He was a hard taskmaster, but at least we knew what we had. God knows what we could get somewhere else. And besides, the little house was ours. It wasn't really ours, of course. The master owned it, like all the houses his sailors lived in.

Father had made an agreement with Master Mowinckel to buy the house after his trip on the Dutch ship. Now we didn't dare mention it. Mother and Father had once talked about how, when the house was theirs, they could sell it and get money to move.

Mother dreamed of moving back to the island at the mouth of the fjord, where she grew up. Far away from the malicious gossip and labor for other people. Father had nothing against it, and I didn't, either. I had nothing but work to look forward to in town, until I became too sick and too old.

The dream of the island at the mouth of the fjord was far away now that Father was gone. But we talked a lot about it anyway.

The conversations stopped when the rumors began to swell.

Good sense warned against the rumors, but both Mother and I entertained secret hopes. Neither of us dared to mention what was making our hands shake and our hearts pound.

The rumors wouldn't stop.

[53

Stronger and stronger they raced through the town, good and bad at the same time: The Dutch ship glitters like gold in the sunset, bulging with treasures! The ship floats, surrounded by a deadly fog, with no sign of life on board. It lies heavy in the water, loaded with misfortune. Monstrous creatures like black birds wade through the blood of the crew they have devoured.

The rumors seethed like caustic fluid.

I couldn't stand listening to them.

With my head hidden in Mother's lap, I stayed with her while she prayed, for the first time. I begged God to put an end to the waiting and bring Father back to us.

*T*he black bird grew out of the darkness, acquired contours, weight, smell. Its wings opened, the tips dragging with a dry, rustling noise.

The bird came nearer, so heavy that its broad breast slapped against the ground. Its breast feathers were stiff and shiny black. They bristled against her. It reached her naked feet, panting with anticipation.

She stared with terror down at the body that was hers—naked, helpless, vulnerable.

The body, stretched out like a cross, with the shiny brown legs and arms tied with thick rope and pinned to the deck.

Slowly it waddled in between her widespread legs. It had plenty of time. For her, time was running out.

The dirty yellow beak opened and she looked into a sea of flames. The bird emitted a hissing sigh, as if taking a deep breath before the attack. The stench enveloped her, forced its way into her mouth and nose, and blinded her.

Senseless with terror, she felt the obese body of the bird wriggle farther up, settle itself on her thighs. The

[57

warmth from the bird's body burned against her skin. Burns that would never disappear.

Its beak pecked at her breasts, cut furrows down across her smooth belly, and burst through the tiny opening to her innermost self.

Like a glowing harpoon, the sharp bird beak tore into her. Over and over again. Long after she had fainted from the pain.

Osuqo woke up, wet with sweat.

She fumbled around in the dark, as far as the rope would reach. Searched for Poq's hand, whimpering and afraid. Finally her fingertips felt the cool warmth of his skin, the comforting small pressure of his fingers—even in sleep.

Only then did the black bird take off and flap away with a heavy beating of its wings. Driven into flight again by his nearness. But it would come back, she knew it would. Not yet, if she could just put her face in his hand. Then she was safe from the bird.

She tensed her abused body into an arc, forced the stiff ropes to give a little. Pain, pain, but nothing was more painful than the nightmares.

Poq's open, sleeping hand received her burning face.

A comforting hollow that locked out the terror, but not the image of her face in her father's dead hand.

Hot tears against cool skin.

She pressed her cheek harder into the sleeping hand.

Where his thumb touched her cheekbone a black, hair-fine tattoo should have adorned her face.

The tattoo would have given her many sons and easy births, a stronger amulet than all the others she wore on the inner pelt under her thick sealskin anorak. The raven skull, the bear tooth, the swan beak, and the sparrow claws were amulets that she had received as gifts at birth and had always carried with her, and she had always taken care of them with reverence.

For as long as she could remember, she had filled the amulets with her most loving thoughts, her best dreams and wishes. Proudly she had felt the power growing for her unborn sons. The power that would carry on the life of her and her family.

That's the way it was before the black bird had landed.

Now she was afraid of the amulets' power.

The foreign beasts had abused her. Forced their way into her and emptied their seed in the space that should have been Poq's and hers.

Now it could never be Poq's, for it was no longer hers either.

It was an atrocity.

She could not remember how many there were.

Only her father's red-haired murderer she could not forget.

That cold blue gaze had held her fast, forced her eyes to stay open while he filled her with his seed. Maybe a hairy monster was growing inside her now. Sucking all nourishment from her body, growing from the power of the amulets, until one day she would give birth to a white monster with the raven's sharp eyes, the strength of the bear, and a murderer's soul. If that was so, then the foreign monsters had robbed her of all life. That which would have come, that which had been. Transformed pride into fear, power into threat, and good into evil. Chained her to them with the unbreakable bond of blood.

The thought was an open wound.

Poq moved, restless.

Her fear had forced its way into his dreams once again.

He slept, but his fingers sent a rhythmic pressure, followed the memories of the violation like a calm pulse.

After the black bird had landed, she no longer had any sense of time.

All time was fear and pain, divided up into dazzling light and suffocating darkness.

In the dazzling light she and Poq lay bound while the foreign ship rocked away from their world.

Then came the time in suffocating darkness, only interrupted by the bright rectangle, high above them, when the deck hatch was opened and food thrown down. The sudden, brilliant rectangle frightened them and they huddled together in the safety outside of the light. Slowly they learned to trust that the light meant food.

Everything changed when the dazzling light became

filled with dark figures that came down into the darkness.

After that, nothing was safe anymore.

Osuqo didn't remember everything, didn't want to remember.

But the violation lived within her, always ready to assault her with images she abhorred:

Poq slung into the darkness, his hands bound behind his
    back
herself naked in the brilliant rectangle, pinned to the deck
coarse hands burned against her breasts
hot breath scorched spots of shame into her face
heavy bodies, flames of pain from the tiny, tight opening
    to her brain
throbbing, endlessly
again, again, again
until her screams hurt their ears
and they stopped them with a filthy rag
the screams that had protected her against the revolting
    moans
mercilessly abandoned to that snorting silence,
suddenly a tone cut through the horrors,
low and sad, stronger and louder.
Poq's song,
like a dazzling light splintering the darkness,
filled her with the mountain plateaus, the winds, the flight
    of the eagles,
the triumph of the soul over the body,
that fragile vessel that is the home of immortality.

"Do you remember," he sang,
"the path to eternity which our ancestors have shown us.
Do you remember, my sister, beloved,
that the power is yours for all eternity
you human being,
child of the past,
mother of the future.
You are us
our suffering and triumph."

She rode the song through the pain and shame, her body hard as wood beneath the moaning beasts.

It lasted a long time, a long time.

Time flowed black around a body that did not exist.

Only Poq's song was real as the beasts got dressed, stomped silently up to the brilliant rectangle.

Her father's murderer bent over her. Stared at her stiff, naked body for a long time.

Disgust and revulsion shone in the cold eyes as if he had coupled with a hideous animal. Shame and rage burst like a bubble inside her.

She wanted to howl with hatred, but no sounds came through the rag in her mouth.

Never, she shouted mutely. Never will you have power over my body and soul! Never will your life take hold inside mine! Only death do we have in common, but your death will be decided by the most evil of spirits. They will chase you past the happiness of the Realm of the Dead, to the tortures of the Realm of the Forsaken. There you will be tortured for eternity with the vain hunt for butterflies—your only nourishment!

She caught the ice-blue gaze, forced his eyes to look at his violation.

In the dazzling light the colors of the violation were garish. She knew that until his death he would see the blood and seed that were slowly trickling out from between her thighs.

In the silence, Poq's song.

A low, threatening sound like the growling of a wounded polar bear.

The red-haired murderer listened, shivered as if he was suddenly freezing.

He bent down abruptly without looking at her, cut her loose from the tight ropes, and rolled her over toward Poq and the darkness.

Quickly, almost frightened, he rushed up toward the light.

The hatch slammed shut and the darkness closed around them.

The weeping had lasted a long time in Poq's arms.

The weeping had loosened the muscles in her body and cleansed the wounds from the violation. But the wounds would not close. They ached without ceasing, even after the weeping changed to a sleep-like stupor.

Then she remembered the time before the black bird had landed.

The time before was sparkling light, full of mighty winds and whipping storms, blue-shimmering winter twilight and pale rose summer nights.

The time before was hard toil, sudden joy, and abrupt sorrow, exhausting hunger waiting for the luck of the hunt, overwhelming joy when the luck turned and a whale surrendered its life and eased the people's hunger, solemn moments with sacrifices to the soul of the dead whale, reverent prayers that the next body of the whale would also one day ease the hunger at the settlement.

The time before was people together, in races, drum dances, songs, and stories about the Moon Man and the Sea Woman, about the world before the pillars of the earth collapsed and humans came.

The time before was familiar and orderly, a steady rhythm of spring, summer, autumn, and winter, beneath sharp shadows from black mountains, on open mountain plateaus, near the foaming sea, or in the frozen silence of the ice-covered fjord.

Time now was a gentle stream without beginning or end, a paralyzing poison that held the soul prisoner in a stiff casing of pain and shame.

Time now slid down into a dark abyss where only terror moved.

She crawled on her stomach in the darkness.

It was hard to move without hands or feet.

Her hands and feet didn't exist any longer. Neither did her eyes, mouth, or face. She could not remember when they ceased to be a part of her. It didn't matter now. The only thing that mattered was getting away from the dangerous darkness where the black bird lurked, ready to bore into her again.

She wriggled farther, farther toward the blue twilight.

There she would float quietly, without body, without pain.

She was awakened by pains like lightning through her body.

Her muscles ached with cramps. Her skin had goose-bumps from the cold.

She must have lain like that for a long time, naked after the violation.

Her fingers moved, cautiously.

Down over her breasts, full of welts from rough fingernails, to her stomach and thighs, covered with caked slime and blood, down to the source of the burning pains, the defiled womb. Warm blood was streaming out, growing into a pool beneath her.

Disgust and terror gripped her.

What had the foreign beasts done! Slashed her body so that all life-force was running out?!

That body, which in another time she had been so proud of, which—supple, soft, and pure—had obeyed her completely, that body she could no longer touch without shame.

Perhaps this foreign body would hold her soul captive forever, prevent her soul's journey to the Realm of the Dead. Perhaps *she* would be the one who would have to eat butterflies in the Realm of the Forsaken for all eternity!

Never!

Panic drove her to her feet. She put on her clothes,

trembling, laboriously, the inner pelt of bird skin, the outer fur, her pants, and finally her *kamiks*. She must hurry, hurry! But she could not leave before she was sure that she had everything! Her fingers, numb and stiff, fumbled for the small bag under the outer skin, made sure that everything was there—her *ulo*, the sinew thread, the needle case, and her amulets— everything she would need in another life.

A new lightning bolt of pain raced through her body and forced her to her knees, gasping, nauseated, faint, even more afraid.

The black bird was moving in the darkness.

The blood flowed even faster.

She had to hurry! Her life was running out.

The light! She had to reach the brilliant rectangle. Behind it lay the sea. Slowly, slowly up the ladder, all her strength gathered to lift the heavy hatch. Sudden, dazzling light cutting into her eyes, sea air filling her lungs. She clenched her teeth against the sobs. There was no time. The blood was running faster, hotter.

Freedom, on the other side of the filthy, icy deck, so far and so near. She didn't have the strength. She had to. She forced her aching body onward. Defied the pain and the blood, which was leaving a wide trail behind her wriggling body. Soon, soon she would sink down in soothing purity to the home of the Sea Woman, where her soul would wander, freed at last from the abused vessel.

Sudden, flaming lightning bolts of pain. Her body, almost up to the railing, lay still.

"Go on!" she pleaded, but her body would not obey anymore.

Her fingers scratched helplessly at the icy deck while steaming blood filled the trail behind her.

The black bird was near.

The dirty yellow beak open in a sea of flames.

Slowly she slipped into burning darkness.

Osuqo had not noticed the two foreigners at the railing.

Didn't hear them yelling to each other, didn't see them running toward her.

They rolled her over onto her back and stared in horror from the pale face to the pool of blood which was growing rapidly.

They growled to each other like angry dogs.

The younger one wanted to throw her overboard. Had already grabbed hold of her lifeless legs.

The older one blocked the way. He growled furiously.

"But in God's name! What have you done?!" he went on, bending over her. "She's bleeding to death after your ravishing! Poor little girl, hardly older than my own daughter! Is there no end to the shame you bring on decent people!"

The younger one winced and snapped shame-facedly: "It's just a heathen creature, a wild female animal! Throw her overboard. We have no use for her."

The older one knelt down next to Osuqo. The look he gave the other man was full of contempt as he said softly: "You would have a great deal to answer for to

Our Lord if she really was an animal. But she's a human being—one of God's unredeemed creatures. You should be grateful for that. It makes your sin a little less!"

His words struck like the lash of a whip.

The older one continued in a milder voice: "Now then! Help me stop the bleeding. Bring boiling water and clean rags. Find the torn sail so we can make a warm bed for her on the deck. She needs light and air. But hurry up, for she's close to death!"

It was cold on the bottom of the sea. She was freezing.

Freezing?

Could she freeze when her body no longer existed?

The thought made her even colder.

Hadn't her soul left her body? How long must it be imprisoned in this hated vessel?

How long must she be alone—outside of the Sea Woman's light, without her father's love?

In despair, suddenly so young and uncertain.

She didn't know enough about the journeys of the souls. But only the shamans knew all the hidden mysteries, all the paths to happiness in the Realm of the Dead. Shaman Aua could not help her now. She had to manage alone.

The pain suddenly penetrated through the despair.

Wild, unbearable, it forced her to surrender.

The pain, the cold were icy-blue like the sea. White glimmers of light and long shadows flickered inside and around her. Faster, faster, and she screamed with terror.

Then warm hands that soothed, dried her tears. A calm voice that whispered tenderly.

Father? Was it Father? Had he waited for her? Hadn't he joined the wandering souls?

Father!

She wanted to fix her gaze on the vague figure bending over her, but she did not have time.

The twilight closed around her with silence and deep-blue movement.

She awakened suddenly, soaking wet and shivering from the cold. A new wave threw her down on the bed of sailcloth.

Around her the storm howled. A soot-black sky was gathering, ready to unleash new lashing bursts of rain and wild squalls. The ship was rolling heavily on high, gray-green waves. Helpless, like an animal in the throes of death.

She realized it at once.

She had not escaped from life. She was still *here*, in the power of the black bird!

A foreign shadow towered above her. A rough voice roared something she didn't understand. Heavy, hairy hands grabbed for her.

The nightmare wasn't over! Everything was going to start again!

Hard bodies, raging pain, shame!

Never.

It would *never* start again!

Senseless with terror, she threw herself at the figure. Saw it stumble, lose its balance on the slippery deck, slide helplessly toward the railing and the mighty swells.

She didn't see the figure disappear in the waves, didn't hear the roars of rage from the foreigners when they discovered that their comrade was gone.

She was already back in the blue silence.

She had clung to the sailcloth bed, half filled with ice-cold water. They bellowed and swore, tore her loose, dragged her across the rolling deck to the hatch.

She fought desperately against them.

I must, *must* go into the foaming sea to Father!

Must not go down in the darkness, where the black bird waited to take its revenge.

But they were too many and too strong.

They threw her down into the darkness again. Tied her up with tight ropes and pinned her to the deck.

But they didn't touch her. Didn't they dare?

She felt a faint flash of triumph. Had she scared them with her attack on the figure that the waves took? She hadn't meant to send the foreigner to his death, just protect herself against their atrocities.

The death of the foreigner was a punishment well-deserved, she thought bitterly.

Then she suddenly remembered the warm hands that had stopped the blood, the strong arms that had tenderly rocked her and eased the pain, and she grew frightened.

Who was he, the one who had healed and comforted her?

It couldn't be one of the foreign beasts, for she knew there was nothing in them but evil. Who was he, then?

Her uneasiness grew as she thought.

Again and again she recalled the hands, warm and soothing, saw the hands stretched out. Beseeching? The thrashing figure who slipped helplessly toward the waves.

Who was he? Who was he? Her thoughts churned, over and over again. The storm raged on. Osuqo lay immovable in the tight ropes when the answer finally came.

Tornaq! The unknown man must have been the helping spirit Tornaq! Perhaps the shaman Aua had found a way to help her after all. Had sent a guide who would lead her from life into death, and to happiness in the Realm of the Dead. Tornaq—disguised as one of the foreigners. That must be the explanation!

This made her despair even greater.

Tornaq—rejected by her, swallowed up by the foaming masses of water. Tornaq could not die. But Tornaq could be mortally wounded!

No other explanation was possible and she was lost.

The darkness around her grew thicker, more threatening.

The black bird and the punishment for her unforgivable sin were waiting in the darkness.

If only she could undo what had been done! But there was no way out now. She could only wait.

Alone in the darkness, staring at her mortal sin which burned with a calm flame that nothing could extinguish.

The storm continued with violent force.

She had given up, let her body roll passively in the ropes which tightened and slackened, tightened and slackened. Her tears ran, ran like rivulets in sand.

Perhaps they would never stop. Perhaps the punishment was never to die but to relive eternally the same sufferings, over and over again.

Osuqo suddenly felt so old, she who had just begun her life. Just like the old, she had no hope, no expectations. But she lacked the wisdom and experiences of the old, and she could not—as they could—nourish herself with memories. Her short life was just an outline in the sand, barely visible before the waves erased it. But her grief, sin, and shame were indelible.

Something moved in the dark, something moved heavily toward her. She heard it quite clearly, for the roaring of the storm had diminished to a steady crash every time the ship's keel struck the waves.

There was no resistance in her. She just waited for whatever must come.

A warm, dry hand fumbled for hers.

Poq!

"Where have you been?"

"I've been on a journey."

The fingers that loosened her ropes were stiff. He struggled to untie the knots.

Poq.

His name raced through her, reached her heart, made it pound.

Poq, Poq, Poq.

They were silent.

Their hands searched, sent signals, built bridges across deep chasms of sorrow and loneliness.

She felt that his face had become bony, like the face of a fully grown man, that his arms were thin and full of scars from blows and beatings, that his body was still aching from the abuse. She felt a pang of rage:

"You have suffered!"

"Not as much as you have, Osuqo."

His voice was as soft as his fingers running across her cheekbone, the bridge of her nose, and her chin.

"You should have had my tattoos here."

The words hurt. She had to swallow for a long time before she could continue talking.

"Tell me about death," she begged.

"Then I must tell you about my wandering," he replied evasively. "Let me tell you about life."

"I know everything about life," she said shortly. "I don't want to know any more."

"But we're *alive*, Osuqo." His voice was compassionate. "We're alive *here and now*. The foreigners have taken our lives, but they haven't given us death. I know because I have inquired in the Realm of the Dead. They don't know us there."

"But . . ." Her hope was thin. "But maybe there is an unknown path to the Realm of the Dead. Perhaps our ancestors do not know about the foreigners' method of killing, or about all their evil. How can they know for certain that . . ."

"Our ancestors know," he said quietly. "They know that life is plaited with sorrow and joy, that life is ruled by unexpected evil. That's why they gave us the magic words and the amulets, not against death but against the living evil. They know everything."

"But, this . . ." she began, fumbling.

"The evil that holds us captive here is alive and much greater than you or I know," he said heavily. "Our ancestors know it and they know our future, but they have no amulets or magic words to give us. We are prisoners in the unknown, evil life. We must fight to free ourselves alone, and we have no shortcuts to freedom or death, no pathways that others have taken before us."

Her fingers touched his lips.

"Do you understand, my love," he said tenderly. "I cannot tell you about death."

"Poq," she said simply.

"Yes, we will do everything together."

Whispering into her palm, he continued: "Do you want to hear the song about the Sea Woman?"

She knew it so well, the proud, beautiful song about the mother of the souls of the sea animals.

"Sing to me, brother."

The song dripped into her like rain on a dry field.

It soothed her sorrow and shame and made her forget for a brief moment the terrible thought—that she had committed an unforgivable sin against Tornaq, and thus set herself outside the protection that the Sea Woman gave all her children.

*T*hunder-heavy clouds with blinding-white edges were drifting rapidly across the sky.

Faster than the black ship was approaching the wharves on the beach side, the Dutch ship that had set out almost a year before. The ship that Mother and I had given up hope of ever seeing again.

"You have to look, Christine!" Henrik's voice was insistent.

But nothing could make me take my eyes off the clouds, let go of that majestic peace, undisturbed by the feverish anticipation of the crowd of people on the wharf that warm spring day.

The clouds would drift on, whether the Dutch ship brought happiness or sorrow, and I would drift with them, high above the excitement and whispered prophecies:

". . . there's plague on board! Only half the crew survived . . . Look how heavy she lies in the water, loaded full of costly treasures . . . No, she's drifting without a rudder, laid waste by the plague . . . God help us! Hasn't this town been punished enough . . ."

On and on they went, the hired hands, the house-

[77

wives, the barbers, the merchants, and all those who had gathered on the wharf when the news of the Dutch ship raced through the town.

Again the rumors had brought them together.

The people of this town, whom the rumors had fooled so many times, who had had to endure so many messages of misfortune, who had seen so many pitiful remnants of proud ships tugged into Vågen. Here they were—the bakers with flour on their hands, the butchers with animal blood in strange patterns on their chest and arms, the tanners enveloped in the stench of rotting hides, the servant girls with whining babies on their arm—torn away from their daily chores by the rumors.

Only Master Mowinckel and the other merchants who had invested their money in the ship had managed to put on their formal black clothes.

I heard them muttering excitedly about the wondrous treasures in the Dutch ship, which would return to them power and privileges and the favor of the King, heard them whispering hatefully that their new wealth would break the power of the foreigners at the wharves, saw how the crowd was infected by their vengeful anticipation, and I felt sick. Their greed was soon greater than the hope of getting the sailors back alive, and it increased in time with the beat of the jugglers' drums.

The clouds drifted.

No longer black with thunder, but mysteriously deep blue, edged with gold and rose. I measured time in drifting clouds.

How much time I had measured in vain this past year!

"Why can't you be happy, too?" Henrik was offended.

I didn't answer.

It wouldn't have done any good anyway, because Henrik was deaf and blind in his learned world. He couldn't see the evil in the joy around us, but I had to protect myself. Defend myself against wallowing in my misfortune, for no one would ever see me cry.

That's why I was staring at the clouds. Letting myself drift along, high above the excitement. As long as I didn't let myself be carried along by the anticipation, the worst could never happen—that the ship was returning from the realm of the dead.

It was a secret pact I had entered into with the heavens, because I knew that black misfortune was heading for the happy town, never so beautiful as now with its colorful houses, towering churches, and green headlands.

If I could only keep the pact, the misfortune would be avoided.

"They're lowering the sails!"

New excitement. Impatiently the people crowded closer together.

The ship must be quite close by now.

"Look!" Like a deep sigh, it rushed through the crowd, so urgent that I lost control for a moment and heard myself pray: "God! Let Father be alive! Let him have my unicorn with him!"

I regretted it at once.

The pact was broken. The clouds drifted away from me.

I was again a helpless girl without the power to keep misfortune away, alone in the crowd that was tensely following the progress of the ship in toward the wharf.

The ship seemed gloomy and silent, despite the men on deck who were making ready to drop anchor.

The heavy bow was damaged, battered by storm and ice, and the sails were shredded. It was a wounded bird that returned home.

Amidships stood the red-haired captain with his hands behind him and his head bowed, stiff and alone.

A powerful shudder went through the wharf when the ship came alongside. A moan that made both the crowd and the jugglers' drums fall silent.

The crew stood on deck, grimy and exhausted.

There was distance between them, as if something evil held them apart. The fear was a cold lump in my stomach. What was wrong?

Again and again I searched through the shabby crew. Could that be all of them?

My eyes, blinded by tears, did not see what I already knew. Father wasn't there!

The captain raised his head. His gaze swept over the crowd, distant as the clouds. For an instant I stared into icy-blue cold.

I didn't need to wait any longer.

The answer was final.

I had to get away, get away at once!

Henrik gripped my arm: "All hope is not lost! Believe me!"

I tore myself loose, for all hope *was* lost. That stupid, vain prayer to God had left me with no defense against the joy of those who received their sons and fathers home again, against the greedy ones who called for their treasures.

I begged to be let through. Couldn't face hearing how Father and the others had lost their lives. There was no hurry now.

I pleaded, hammering with my fists on the bodies forcing me closer and closer to the ship. They were intoxicated with joy and excitement, heedless of anything but their own desires.

"The treasures! We want to see the treasures!"

"Yes, the treasures, Captain! Bring them up on deck!" Master Mowinckel's voice was authoritative. The crowd willingly let him pass. Eager hands helped him aboard. But they wouldn't let *me* get away.

"Let me go! Please!" I cried. To no avail.

Then Henrik was suddenly there. Grabbed my head, pressed it against his jacket.

"Go ahead and cry, Christine. Don't look, I'll tell you about it."

As the terrible disappointment finally broke inside me, Henrik whispered:

"They're opening the hatches, bringing up piles of reindeer skins and fox pelts—they're white and beautiful—several heavy polar-bear skins—those are probably worth a lot of money—heaps of dried fish and meat, several dozen fine walrus tusks and . . . this will secure Father a good income . . . barrels of seal blubber. Here is a lot of expensive lamp oil! No wonder Father is smiling so contentedly."

He stopped.

I snuffled and dried my eyes.

"Look now, Christine. It's so beautiful!" Henrik said breathlessly.

It had become completely silent on the wharf. People held their breath while the sailors carefully carried the treasures over to Master Mowinckel and put them down as if they were made of the most fragile glass.

They were incredibly beautiful. Two gleaming spears pointing at the sky, with fine spiral fluting, pale rose in the sunshine. Two enormously valuable horns from the timid unicorns.

The crowd gasped in amazement.

Master Mowinckel gave a trembling sigh of happiness, for now he had become even richer.

I swallowed my bitterness. Never had I felt poorer than at that moment.

I couldn't look. The beautiful horns mocked all my dreams. But the wall of people around me was denser than ever. Hungry eyes in motionless faces hemmed me in, forcing me to look at the ship.

Something caught my eye. Something quite different from the smug Master Mowinckel and the cool captain.

Four sailors on their knees next to an open hatch were struggling with something large, soft, and tremendously alive, in gray fur, something that resisted with all its might, growling and biting. But to no avail, for the sailors had the superior strength, and dragged the live gray thing between them.

Suddenly, a piercing, drawn-out howl, and the sailors swore and cursed, thrashing at soft bodies.

A gasp of horror went through the crowd. What was this? Wild animals? Or the notorious devils from the icy land? More howling and snarling, blows and kicks, then the sailors had reached the captain. They threw their burden down at his boots.

It was totally still as the captain raised his heavy whip. Again and again it whistled down toward those soft backs.

It lasted a long time, whistling whiplashes and faint moans.

Finally the captain lowered his whip. The bodies lay motionless.

I felt sick to my stomach.

The crowd was silent.

The captain growled an order. The sailors lifted two fur-clad creatures, who staggered and were about to fall. A new sharp order from the captain, and the sailors raised their fists to strike.

Then a hissing sound came from one of the creatures, low and threatening like a warning.

The fists dropped, and the sailors backed up a step. Master Mowinckel pressed against the railing in terror.

Suddenly alone, the creatures stood with heads high and black fearless eyes.

Horror swept through the crowd.

They weren't wild animals at all!

"It's . . . but they look like us!" I heard myself say.

Incredulous muttering spread all around me. Two creatures, obviously a male and a female. Even though both were short, one of them was taller and stockier. Their faces were deep golden, their hair blue-black and thick. The male's hair was gathered in long tassels by his ears. The female's flowed freely to her waist.

Their clothes were of grayish-brown skins. The male had a tanned shirt, fur pants, and high boots. The female's shirt was longer and tapered to a point in front and back. She also had fur pants and high boots.

They moved, softly and gracefully.

The crowd gasped.

The female took a step forward, the crowd a step back.

Suddenly I was alone.

The female's eyes met mine, for a long time.

I saw deep sorrow, but no fear. I saw a plea for mercy, but not for help. Black and proud was that gaze, which came from another world, and for an instant it touched a faded dream. A fleeting shadow with spots of sunshine on its pelt, the beautiful unicorn I would never catch.

"Father is dead. He's never coming back." The sorrowful voice was inside my head, as my terrified voice was in hers.

"What do you want with me?"

"You know me. We share a fate." Calmly.

Suddenly, black wide-open eyes and flashing lightning of pain.

The sailors grabbed her arms, twisted them behind her back, forced her to her knees. Then the male. Brutally the proud necks were bowed. But the male hissed again, more threateningly, and it ignited the loathing of the crowd. It grew into a shout:

"Captain! You've brought us devils . . . heathen creatures . . . why? They'll spread black magic and misfortune . . . bring God's judgment down on us . . . why, Captain? Why?"

"They must be punished for their terrible misdeeds!" thundered the captain. "They scoffed at God and attacked our people! Don't you see how many good men are missing?"

"Why didn't you throw the devils into the sea? Why did you bring them here? Hasn't our town suffered enough?"

The captain leaned forward, grabbed the female's long, shiny hair, and brutally jerked her head up.

"Look closely at this heathen female beast, good people. In His great mercy God has given it human form, but she is a devilish murderer! In cold blood she killed sailor Claus Pedersøn, who in his goodness was treating her for an illness she herself was responsible for!"

I was about to fall. Dizzy with old grief and new knowledge.

Was it true? True!

Hands grabbed me. Henrik whispered: "Don't believe everything!"

The captain thundered on. His knuckles around her black hair were white. Her golden-brown throat was arched like a bow. With a single little snap the captain could break her neck.

His eyes flashed as he turned to the sailors: "Tell them the truth!"

But the sailors hesitated and turned their eyes away.

The captain's voice was like a whiplash: "Is this not the truth?"

They nodded slowly, reluctantly. The distance between them increased. They found no ally in the lie, just greater shame and loneliness. But the sailors were hiding something. Something terrible. About Father's death? What had happened? What was the truth? How . . . how . . . how . . . My head ached as though it would burst, again and again the voice repeated: "Father is dead. He's never coming back. We share a fate, we share a fate, we share a fate . . ."

I sank to the ground, my strength gone. The hands that held me were shaking. Henrik's voice was hoarse, furious: "Don't listen anymore, Christine!"

Far away the captain bellowed: "Good citizens! What do these devils deserve?"

"Punishment! Punishment!" howled the crowd.

"I turn over the murderers to your just punishment!" His words flamed through the crowd like fire in dry grass, drove them closer together, closer to the side of the ship. Hands reached out greedily toward the two.

"Give us the devils! Burn them at the stake . . . burn them!"

The words hammered in my ears, made my heart pound as if possessed by horror, as if *I* were the one the flaming hatred was directed toward.

"We share a fate, share a fate." They must not do this to her! To us! No matter what she was guilty of!

The captain held her above his head, ready to throw her to the crowd thirsty for revenge.

"No!" I moaned, but my voice was drowned out in the clamor.

"They're about to commit a terrible sin, driven by fear and the captain's lies!" said Henrik. "This must not happen, Christine!"

He shouted: "*Stop!*"

A moment later he stood on deck beside the captain and his unfortunate victims. His figure was as awkward as always in the clothes that were much too tight, but his voice was unrecognizably forceful:

"Stop! In God's name, good citizens! Do you mean to attack another man's property? Punish and burn my father's creatures? What the captain is asking you to do is a crime!"

It was as if he had poured water on a bonfire. The shouting ceased. In the silence I heard the calm waves lapping against the side of the ship. The crowd was listening attentively to the authoritative young man.

The captain dropped his arms, let the female fall to the deck like a doll. His face was expressionless, but his eyes glowed with a hatred that frightened me.

"Father," shouted Henrik, turning toward Master Mowinckel. He came closer, shaking and pale. "The heathens are your property, aren't they? Like the horns and the barrels of seal blubber?"

His father nodded, swallowing several times, unable to utter a sound.

The crowd looked on, tensely.

"In that case, can you allow this man"—Henrik pointed at the captain—"who is in *your* service, to do as he likes with *your* property?"

Restless muttering in the crowd. Master Mowinckel regained his power of speech. "Of course it is *my* property"—he cast a quick glance at the merchants and the shipowners on the wharf—"*our* property!"

They nodded in agreement.

"And *we* and no one else will decide if the creatures shall be punished for murder and misdeeds which the captain alleges they have committed."

Another glance at the merchants before he continued, feeling superior: "But we have law and justice in our civilized town, and they shall prevail—even for insane heathens."

More muttering from the crowd and nods of agreement from the black-clad men.

"For these good citizens are also men of law, and are empowered to condemn to the stake or to some punishment. No mob can do that by itself!" he concluded decisively.

"Well spoken, honored Father!" said Henrik in admiration. "And as good Christians our first duty is to turn these heathens to God, as it is our duty to let learned men study the customs and ways of the godless, so that our King can obtain useful knowledge about his realms in the north, those which still remain in the darkness of ignorance!"

Master Mowinckel was proud of his son's clever words—that was easy to see. It was a master full of authority who turned to the attentive gathering on the wharf: "Go back to your work, good people! And we shall attend to our property and law and justice!"

"Rejoice over those who have returned, and grieve over the dead," added Henrik quietly.

The tension was broken, the rage and vengefulness dissolved, and the captain no longer had power over the crowd.

Relief filled me like a fresh spring breeze fills a stuffy room. Gone was the sorrow, the fear, the terrible question about Father's death, for a moment. Then I saw the captain's face. Pale beneath his red hair, contorted in an odd smile. With a cowed look in which something evil smoldered. Suddenly afraid, I thought: Why did he want the creatures turned over to the wrath of the people, to the stake and burning? Did he want to hide something by their death?

And the doubt surfaced, speaking softly: What if he acted out of righteous wrath, wanting to avenge your father's death?

I found no answer, only nagging doubt and deep, deep emptiness.

"Give the sailors leave, Captain!" ordered Master Mowinckel, and the captain obeyed at once.

The crew jumped lightly over the railing, as if they couldn't get away fast enough from the black ship. They were welcomed with open arms and smiling faces.

On the empty deck only the captain, the master, and Henrik were left, and the two sailors who had had orders to lay the creatures in chains.

Around me billowed the joy of reunion. Stiff and silent I watched the sailors kick and strike the creatures and put them into heavy chains as if they were dangerous bulls. Like a faint echo I heard the words: "We share a fate," more sorrowful than ever. I wondered if I would ever understand *how*.

The wharf was almost empty of people.

The jugglers had led the sailors and their large, happy following up into town. I could hear that it was not far to the taverns and beer halls. Tonight the town would celebrate its returning sailors and Master Mowinckel's treasures.

Only a compact group of weeping women and little children kept me company, and a few miserable paupers and beggars.

There are no alms to be had here today, I thought wearily, and none tomorrow, either. Soon many of the women would rush along alleys and streets on the same errand as the beggars. The youngest and prettiest would probably have to find a place in the brothels for the foreign tailors and shoemakers. There they would come to earn the contempt of the town and life's mercy as long as they were young and free of wrinkles. After that, the road to death by starvation was short.

Their little children would soon be gone from the marketplaces and streets, sent away as wards of the crowded inland parishes or the meager fishing villages far out by the mouth of the fjord. It was a miserable life for widows and orphans.

God's mercy and compassion, I thought bitterly, and at once felt a pang of conscience. Hadn't I heard Pastor Absalon thunder again and again from the pulpit that misfortunes were *not* the work of the good Almighty God, but the work of Satan and his thousand little devils, who had entrenched themselves everywhere in human life, and as soon as God dozed they would come out and besmirch His glory with their evil deeds.

"Were You dozing, God, when Father was lost?"

Father, who had placed his life in God's hands.

Could God have regrets?

I didn't know the answer, but without humility I demanded that God regret the lives that were taken and the misfortunes that followed.

The spring wind suddenly turned biting cold.

I shivered.

Mother and I were luckier than many others, in spite of everything. We had shelter and work, as long as we bowed our heads and kept our mouths shut.

It was worse for others.

The little flock of women huddled together, craning their necks. They reminded me of grieving cormorants turned toward the sea. At the farthest end of the wharf, a thin little girl was kneeling. Her hands were raised above her head. Slowly bluebells and dandelions drifted down into the filthy water.

"Christine!"

Confident Henrik, no longer the stuttering, blushing young boy. "Come here!"

Not that! Not on board that hateful ship, like walking on Father's grave! My feet wouldn't obey the voice of reason: Remember your place! Remember that you're luckier than a lot of others! The words sounded like mockery as I slowly, unwillingly, forced myself to obey orders. Father's death was present. I felt it as soon as I set foot on the deck. Who was responsible? I found no answer in the stone face of the captain or in the creatures who lay bundled up like pigs ready for slaughter.

Father and son standing next to each other, with the same thing in mind:

"Christine, would you . . ." pleaded Henrik.

"I command you!" his father broke in, annoyed. "It's not a matter of what you *want* to do, my girl, but what you *must* do!"

My eyes met Henrik's. He was imploring me, but I did not have the strength to understand. All I could think about was how exhausted I was and how greatly I longed to get away from the resounding question.

"You will guard and look after these godless creatures while the High Court investigates their misdeeds, while learned men study them, and"—he took a deep breath—"while I find out whether they can be sold for good money in the King's city, where people are amused by all sorts of monsters and repulsive skin colors."

Henrik opened his mouth, horrified, but his father stopped him with an icy look.

"As you quite rightly said yourself, my son, the creatures are *my* property. I will do with them what I like; there's nothing more to be said about it!"

God! I thought unhappily. Were You dozing when

Your unredeemed souls were captured? Do You see now what fate awaits them?

I caught Henrik's eye, begged him to spare me this. He shook his head faintly, sympathetically. Silently he mouthed some solace: You won't be alone. I am with you.

But I could not, would not be the creatures' guard. Would it do any good to beg Master Mowinckel for mercy?

His back was turned to me. With his elegant walking stick he was poking at the two bundles of fur. The female lay motionless in her chains, staring with glazed eyes into another world. The male gave a start and looked up at me. Again that deep, black gaze which was soothing and disturbing at the same time.

They were foreign and unknown, beings from the icy desolation of Meta Incognita, perhaps even dangerous. But I could no longer believe that they had caused my father's death.

"Spare me this," I whispered, almost inaudibly. The broad black silk back did not move. What did he care about the grief of a pitiful servant girl, a grief that would return again and again at the sight of the living proof of Father's death?

"All right," I said quietly. What would Mother and I have to look forward to if I said no? Not much more than that little flock of cormorants at the farthest end of the wharf.

*I*t was terribly hot.

The heat clung to her body and made the burden even heavier.

She could feel that she had been carrying heavy things all day.

Her stomach told her that it was soon time for rest and food. It was growling with hunger.

The landscape around the wanderers from the settlement was open and hospitable. Rolling heath, interspersed with lush fields of cotton grass. Red and green, dry and wet, constantly alternating all the way up to the distant mountains, rose-brown with sharp shadows in the afternoon sun.

Between the mountains and the wanderers lay the great inland lake, smooth and still. On the shore they would rest, before they put the women's boats into the water and rowed to the foot of the mountains in the bright summer night.

"It's not far now," Osuqo comforted herself.

She looked at the big women's boats rocking in front

of her on the shoulders of her father and the other men. The boats looked so ungainly and big in this scrubby landscape. But they were different in the water when they glided soundlessly forward like broad-breasted birds. She thought of cool, rushing water against her fingertips, and the silence. Every little sound came echoing back from the silent mountains. As if the visitors had to be reminded to show respect for the infinite silence.

The silence was absolute here in the interior, only broken by the cries of the ravens and the much rarer warning signals of the eagles. Completely different than on the coast, where the restless sea always reminded the people that nature is omnipotent.

The silence here was gentle, free of the fear of sudden death.

She heard only the rhythmic, soft sloshing of the *kamiks* in the heather, and the impatient whimpering of the dogs as they scampered among the silent wanderers from the settlement.

It was important to conserve your energy in order to endure the wearisome journeys. There would always be time enough for songs and stories after they reached the summer encampment.

Fine, thought Osuqo. Then my thoughts will wander undisturbed in the silence.

It was strange to feel as free as a bird while struggling up the hill with a heavy burden on her back. She would have liked to be a bird, floating above the countryside and mountains, hiding in the clouds and swooping down abruptly into the sea for food. So much easier than sitting still for hours and waiting for the seal to appear.

Yes, a bird. If only she didn't get so dizzy in the high mountains.

Her thoughts came back down to earth again. She, who would soon be grownup, shouldn't be fantasizing about being a bird! She ought to think about sensible things, like salmon fishing, or reindeer hunting, or berry picking . . .

"Osuqo! Stop!"

"No, Little Brother! Not now, we can't stop. Can't you see we're far behind the others?"

"But there's something here!"

"There's *always* something, Little Brother. Come on, or Father will be mad at us both!"

"Yes, but I saw something!"

"What *is* it then, you troublemaker?"

She had already given in. It never did any good to stop Little Brother when there was something he wanted.

The weary muscles in her body protested when she turned and followed the small, chubby figure which was jumping lightly from tuft to tuft in the field of cotton grass. He stopped suddenly and bent down. She almost fell over his round, fur-clad bottom.

"Look what I found, Osuqo! Isn't it pretty?"

He was kneeling down in the soggy peat ridge. Between his small brown hands she caught a glimpse of a downy bird's head with big black eyes. The tiny beak opened bravely.

He lifted the young bird up carefully, higher, toward the sky.

"Don't be afraid, little bird. I'll take care of you until you're grownup and able to fly with the others," he whispered.

Osuqo sank down beside him.

She could never keep her heart from melting at the sight of that round, serious face with the lively eyes! She looked at his hands cupped so tenderly around a creature even smaller and more defenseless than himself, and she was almost breathless with love. She could get so angry because he was so stubborn, but she loved his courage and his compassion.

"What's wrong, Osuqo? Are you tired?"

She swallowed and nodded.

"But I couldn't have left it behind, could I?"

No, that wouldn't have been like her brother.

He tilted his head and stared at her. There was a golden glow deep inside his warm eyes.

"Are you mad, Osuqo?"

Mad? Could anyone be really mad at him?

Suddenly she realized that this was exactly how she would always remember him. Happy and free in a wide-open landscape beneath a golden-colored sky.

"I'll carry it for you," she said quietly. "Put it carefully up in my hood. It will be safe there."

Little Brother smiled gratefully. He got busy making a soft nest of grass for the young swan in the hood of her anorak. She sat still while he worked. If she knew him, he was probably searching for some extra-fat insects that the young bird could eat during the journey. That's the way he was.

The long line of wanderers was growing smaller and smaller in the vast landscape.

She felt strangely refreshed and calm. It wasn't so hot anymore, either.

Finally he was finished and she could put her burden in place on her back again and carefully arrange the hood with the young bird on top.

They walked on.

"Do you know that it's a young swan you've found?" she said.

"How wonderful!" he said happily. "They're so beautiful when they fly."

The wanderers had almost reached the inland lake.

Perhaps Father would be angry, but that didn't matter now. He, too, knew that there were precious times you had to hold on to. Moments that made life so good that it hurt.

"Don't cry anymore, Osuqo. Don't let them see you crying."

It was not a plea from Poq. It was an order.

Osuqo swallowed her tears immediately.

He was right. The humiliations as prisoners of the foreigners were plentiful enough without her adding to them.

Proud Poq. He did everything to preserve the dignity that made their race deserving of the name "the People."

Osuqo was ashamed at her own weakness.

When the foreigners on the ship had tied them up like dangerous animals, Poq had stood with raised head and a stony expression. She had surrendered to rage, screamed and bit.

Poq had calmly let himself be dragged to the cart on the dock. She had fought against them, spit and hissed.

Poq had sat with his back erect and his eyes closed during the whole terrible trip through the town with the gaping, gawking crowds of people, to the building where they were locked up in a dark, stinking room. She had lain trembling in the bottom of the cart, wept and begged for mercy from all the fearful terrors.

In her world—the world of the People—no one was treated so miserably, not even the lowliest land animal. In her land, animals were hunted for food, but their souls were treated with the greatest respect. In her land, people and animals lived in freedom. There existed only the freedom of life or the freedom of death.

In the foreigners' world she had learned to know imprisonment and new pain. She feared that she still had much to learn.

What did they want with her and Poq?
She couldn't figure it out.
They came with smoldering torches in their hands. Their faces shone white with revulsion mixed with fear. They treated Poq and her as if they were objects, not human beings. Touched their hair, their teeth, their skin, their clothes without respect or sympathy.

Did they have souls, these foreigners?
She couldn't believe that souls were housed in so

much evil and coldness. The thought of what was in store for them at the hands of the foreigners was even more terrifying after that.

But she wasn't raped anymore.

The red-haired monster with the ice-blue eyes was gone.

He disappeared the day they arrived in the foreigners' world, the day the girl with the pale hair and the withered arm became their guard. The red-haired monster and the black bird would never vanish completely. They had taken up residence in her forever, hidden in a chamber deep inside. Always ready to be conjured up when she least expected it.

When the straw on the floor of the dungeon rustled dryly, Osuqo would hear the black bird dragging its unfolded wings across the planks of the deck toward her stretched-out body. Then she would be filled with terror again and want to escape. But where, and how?

Dark figures moved outside the door day and night. She heard the clank of weapons. She knew that they were many and they would stop her, harm and humiliate her even more, but not grant her the freedom of death. Outside the prison there was a dangerous world that made her sick with fear. She could never escape alone, and Poq would not go with her.

"The time is not ripe," he said simply, and pointed at the iron chains on their hands and feet. Heavy, tight chains that forced them to hop like injured crows to the food that the pale girl put inside for them.

She knew that Poq was right.

Osuqo found another way to escape, farther and farther into the world of the People from which she had been kidnapped.

Her memories grew sharper and clearer. Especially of her little brother.

Her memories were like a sun-warmed stone, worn by the waves, a stone in her hands, giving her solace and something to hold on to.

Osuqo removed herself from the prison and the foreigners.

She no longer saw the soot-black walls, no longer noticed the pale girl who sat motionless in a corner and just stared at them. She ignored the thin boy who tried to talk to them, and the man with the fat stomach who pinched her as if she were a newly slaughtered seal.

With indifference she swallowed the revolting food that the girl brought. The day she became ill, she felt only relief. She lost herself in dreams of the thawing of the ice in the bay and waited, for freedom.

Poq refused to be broken by their imprisonment.

He defied the heavy chains, examining every detail of the dungeon. He stroked the broad timbers in the walls—bigger than any he had ever seen—studied the torch that could burn so long, and listened for hours to the voices outside the door.

In this way he formed images of the foreigners. He reported eagerly to Osuqo:

". . . it's an older, heavyset man. His voice is whining . . . probably very sick . . . while the other one with the light step also has a lot to complain about, you can hear it in his voice . . . Now they're eating . . . ugh! what a disgusting smell!"

She refused to listen or to smell anything.

". . . something's coming . . . probably the rolling sled, the one they drove us over here in, Osuqo. I think I understand some words of their language now, listen: . . . that means *water* . . . that probably means *food*, and that must mean *thank you* . . ."

"I don't want to listen!" Osuqo interrupted. "Their voices are like angry dogs snapping at each other."

"That's what *you* say," said Poq sadly.

He moved close to her.

"Don't flee from me, Osuqo. You're the only one I have, the only one who can help me through these trials. I need you."

"I need you, too, Poq," she said shamefully.

"We are one now, more than brother and sister," said Poq. "Help me find out what the foreigners want with us, then we'll find out how we can escape from them."

"There is no sense to what the foreigners do. They're just insane, evil spirits!" she said angrily.

"You don't think the girl with the withered arm and the sad eyes is an evil spirit, do you? Or the boy who is trying to understand our words?"

She didn't answer.

"They are *human beings* just like us, but not of our race," he said.

Osuqo shuddered.

"It's true! Even though you don't want to hear it," he said insistently. "You know the old stories about the way human beings were created. Other people existed before our race. You also know that foreign ships have visited the land of the People for many generations and have traded iron and wood for skins and horns. The old stories say nothing about where the foreigners came from. Now we know that there exists a world outside *our* world, with people who look like us but who are not of our race. We've discovered something that none of our people knows, Osuqo! It's our task to gather all the knowledge we can and take it back to the land of the People."

"That's quite a large task and an honorable burden you're placing upon us," she said at last. Her voice was thin and afraid.

He stroked her hand quickly.

Perhaps it was wrong of him to take away from her the hatred with which she protected herself. The foreigners had been much more brutal toward her than toward him. There had been times when he doubted whether she could survive the torture and the shame. But there was no other way. The hatred made her blind and deaf, and he had to count on her seeing and hearing.

"The shaman's trials are both numerous and difficult," he said quietly. "But the trials are the only light in the darkness of the mysteries. None of our race has encountered trials as great as those we must endure, but we'll manage, won't we?"

She nodded. "They are the only path to freedom," she said.

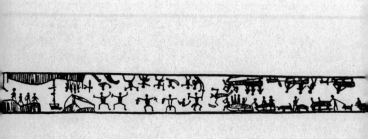

*T*he unicorn was back in my dreams. Distinct, alive, the way it was when I thought it was the symbol of my happy future.

But everything was different now. The dreams, too. A new, foreign longing had crept in, a longing I had no words for, but which was there inside me every morning like pent-up tears.

It began after I became the guard for the unhappy creatures. How I detested the burden Master Mowinckel had placed on me! What an ingenious punishment: the victim who guards the victims.

Even now, when the bitterness stung me—I still couldn't think of those two as *guilty*. I could only see them as *victims*, in the same situation as me, only with a worse fate in store for them.

As their guard, I felt like a traitor. Against *what* I didn't really know, and I didn't have the energy to find out. I only knew that I detested the daily walks to the town hall where they were held captive, hated the guards' shameless talk about the creatures, especially about the female, hated to see the male limping restlessly around the dungeon while the female sat motionless and stared into space with empty eyes.

It shamed me to see hunger force them to eat the half-rotten fish and the moldy bread I brought them. It tortured me to see them be poisoned. I poured out my troubles to Henrik, but it was as if he didn't hear me. Not until the creatures got sick did he understand, and he was furious.

After a bitter quarrel between Henrik and Master Mowinckel which echoed throughout the house, the creatures were no longer fed with kitchen garbage. Master Mowinckel reluctantly gave in to his son and decided that they could have fresh food. But only innards and leftovers, for that was suitable food for wild animals, he said.

But I sneaked a fresh crust of bread to them whenever I dared. There was little more I could do, except hope that they would get their freedom back someday. But that was a meager hope, considering the mood that prevailed in the town.

Henrik didn't notice a thing, absorbed as he was in his great discovery and his learned books.

The creatures could talk, he had discovered. Of course it was a language neither he nor I could understand, but they did talk—*wanted* to talk with him. It had taken a long time. He had sat with them for days on end, repeating the same words over and over in a calm voice without result.

Then the male suddenly stopped his restless pacing, sat down in front of Henrik with his chained arms crossed, and listened. But the female continued to stare straight ahead, at a point I knew was not in that room. Henrik had found some hope, had kept searching eagerly for some way they could understand each other, with signs and gestures, words from our language and Icelandic, the language which sounded so strangely similar to ours.

The male had listened for a long time, silent and unapproachable. Then the change came. Henrik drew a human being. He pointed at me, himself, the drawing, and them.

"People," he said, over and over again.

The male's eyes lit up, suddenly alive, proud. He pointed from himself to the female, to Henrik and me.

"Inuit!" he exclaimed.

"People!" repeated Henrik, elated.

"Inuit—people—Inuit!"

"People—Inuit—people!"

Happy as two young boys who have discovered a new game, they flung words back and forth to each other, rejoicing over being able to understand. The female stayed out of their game for a long time, then she joined in. First reluctantly, then more eagerly. Their language was incomprehensible, but pleasantly soft and musical.

I couldn't take part in their game, but I followed it. From the darkest corner of the dungeon, where I sat and pondered something Henrik had said. "They're *people*, Christine! Like you and me! Of the same species, but not the same color!"

"Don't let anyone hear you!" I begged him. "Not now!"

Henrik had looked at me uncomprehendingly, as if

he didn't realize that it was dangerous and heretical talk. But he himself had heard Pastor Absalon thunder from the pulpit that the godless and heathen were not real human beings!

Yes, Henrik knew, but he didn't care. For his head was full of the discoveries he had made during long sleepless nights in the little room filled with books.

He paid no heed to the smoldering madness in the town. Not even the change that had come over his own father. But *I* noticed it, and was to feel the consequences.

Master Mowinckel, who first had been proud as a rooster over the strange creatures he was going to sell to the highest bidder in the King's city, had recently been scared to death whenever they were mentioned.

I knew why he snarled angrily when anyone mentioned the creatures, because I had heard Madame's nagging and complaining. She hadn't seen the two unfortunate creatures, but she was convinced that they were Satan's messengers.

It was a monstrous thing, she nagged, that the master protected two murderous wild animals. It was a mockery of God, to the great contempt of the public and the family's deep shame. Especially now, when his daughter was soon to celebrate her wedding to the powerful Dr. Abraham. How *could* the master risk so much for the sake of two heathens?

The complaints pricked like needles, and the master was surely scared enough already.

He had no doubt noticed that people in town were of the same opinion as Pastor Absalon, that the heathens were a shame and a disgrace to piety and decency. And he knew that even worse things were smoldering—the fear that the heathens would strike the town with maleficium—black magic and evil deeds.

From the pulpit Pastor Absalon fed the fire of the smoldering fear: "God's judgment is nigh! Woe to him who thinks that God will turn a blind eye to violations against His holy name and kingdom!" he thundered, and the congregation groaned in terror. In the front pews sat the sheriff, the bailiff, and the councilor. They nodded solemnly at the pastor's words, while the rumors grew like weeds in the marketplaces.

People swore that the two heathens had hooves instead of feet. Several people had seen them flying on black wings above the roofs of the town at night. Many knew of cows that had gotten sick, or children who had contracted fever.

Witchcraft hysteria ran rampant in our town, for the first time in years. This time the object of suspicion wasn't a gruff old woman or a vengeful husband, but two unknown beings from an equally unknown world nobody cared about. There was no one in town who was willing to stand up for the two wretches—who would swear that they were *not* witches. The creatures were completely alone and without protection from the hatred that was growing stronger every day. And even worse: the suspicions also turned against me.

A cripple like me isn't used to kindness from people. That had never bothered me. But the fact that people now shunned me as if I were in league with Satan himself made me sick with fear.

I had detested the trips to the town hall, but now

every single day became a true nightmare. I started sneaking out long before it got light, while the town was still asleep, and didn't return home until the town had gone to bed. In this way I avoided meeting anybody, but it didn't stop the gossip, or the madness that was drawing closer and closer. I knew that it could break out into action at any time—directed at the creatures, and at me. For if I wasn't in league with the devils from the unknown world, then I ought to be able to bear witness against them. I was the only person who was with them every day, who knew their every movement.

This is exactly the way Master Mowinckel talked to me the evening he was waiting for me in the hall outside the kitchen, when I came sneaking back from the town hall.

First I felt sick from anger, then from fear.

Master Mowinckel was even more scared than I was. He was shaking and sweating as he muttered incoherently about the evil deeds that people said the creatures had committed.

"Maleficium!" he whispered, and the word sent a chill down my spine.

That terrible word which described the worst of all human crimes, for which there was no milder punishment than burning at the stake.

Master Mowinckel had decided to ask the bailiff to bring the creatures before the court, accused of murder and witchcraft. In this way he could free himself of every suspicion that he was in league with Satan and his servants, and now he wanted me to do likewise.

"Save yourself, Christine!" he said over and over again. "Just swear that you have seen them fly to Bloksberg, the Witches' Mountain!"

At first I was speechless, and that was probably just as well. Otherwise, I would have told him what I thought of him. When I regained my tongue, I only stammered: "It's not true . . . None of it is true . . . They aren't witches . . ."

"Then you refuse to help your master? All right! You have only yourself to blame!" he snarled, and disappeared.

That night I pounded so long on Henrik's door that he finally opened it, exhausted and sleepless from studying day and night.

"Henrik!" I begged him. "Listen to what I have to tell you!"

His weary face lit up. He pulled me into the room, over to the piles of books and papers, as he talked excitedly: "Nobody else but you must hear about this, Christine! I've found the final proof . . ." He rustled through his papers without noticing that I was crying in fright and begging him to listen.

"You know that the sagas tell about Norwegians who crossed the sea to Iceland and then sailed to Greenland? They settled down there and lived well. For a long time news came from that distant land, but then it stopped. There hasn't been any news for a hundred years, so people have forgotten that they existed . . ." He searched frantically through his papers

[117

and finally found what he was looking for. "But now I know that the two foreigners are descendants of the proud Norwegians who once sailed off to the west . . . yes, I can actually prove it, for they understand Icelandic, after all . . . You heard them yourself, didn't you?"

For the first time he looked straight at me, and I stopped crying from sheer dismay. To think that he could sit quietly in his room and play with heretical thoughts while the death sentence hung over their heads!

"Henrik!" I moaned.

"Do you realize what my discovery means, Christine?" he said, almost accusingly. "That it is people of our own race we're holding captive and treating like wild animals! What a terrible disgrace!"

Disgrace? I thought. What could be worse than the threat hanging over them, which he didn't even want to hear about?

"Will you please listen, Henrik!" I screamed. "It's not important *who* they are, or *where* they come from! They're going to die soon, no matter what!"

Finally—finally he listened to me, and he was furious.

No one slept a wink in the house that night.

The heated quarrel between Henrik and his father kept everyone awake.

"Murder and maleficium?! Are you out of your mind, Father, raising such terrible false accusations against them? And why are you dragging poor Christine into this insanity? Are there no limits to . . ." Henrik roared.

"You heard the captain's testimony yourself!" his father roared back.

"And you would trust the word of *that* man?" Henrik scoffed. "You, who yourself caught him trying to cheat you out of three barrels of blubber!" He took a deep breath and continued, triumphantly: "You heard for yourself how the sailors shied away from accusing anyone of murder. Besides, the captain accused the poor wretches of murder, never of witchcraft! Where did that accusation come from? Where's your evidence?"

It was silent for some time.

"I have given my word that they shall stand trial," his father said sullenly.

"To *whom* have you given your word, and what proof do you have?" Now it was Henrik on the attack.

There was another long silence.

"*Who*, Father?" Henrik's voice was heavy with anger.

His father refused to answer.

"It can only be your honorable son-in-law, Dr. Abraham, who's trying to save his own skin, or my dear mother, who always worries about the slightest blemish on her reputation. Or . . ." he continued, more slowly, ". . . it's your good friends the merchants and shipowners. The ones who are also on the court and who will judge the accused."

It was so quiet it seemed that the entire house was holding its breath.

"It's the all-powerful merchants you've given your

word to, isn't it? The ones who have the law in their hands. Then the judgment has been made in advance, Father! Even though there isn't a shred of evidence to convict them with!"

"The heathens have to answer for their deeds like everyone else." Master Mowinckel's voice was weaker, a little hesitant.

Henrik was quick to continue: "You have only that devious captain's word that the creatures are guilty of murder, and that's not much proof. But can you, as the honorable and God-fearing man you are, justify, for the peace of your own soul, entering a charge of witchcraft against these helpless foreigners?"

In the silence that followed I heard Master Mowinckel's heavy breathing. Henrik's voice was earnest, imploring:

"In the name of reason and the righteous God! Don't do it, Father! Think of what misfortunes you would set in motion if you turned loose a whole new witch-hunt! Just think of poor Christine, whom you must either accuse along with them or force to bear false witness against them."

In the darkness outside the door I nodded. My tears fell softly onto my tightly clasped hands. My fate was also being decided in there.

"All right," his father said suddenly. "I'll admit you're right about the charge of witchcraft. There's no proof, even though the town is seething with rumors and fear. But . . ." Master Mowinckel paused, then continued in a firm voice: ". . . they have to stand trial for the murders! After all, I've . . ." He broke off, and there was an ominous silence.

"Well, Father. You'll probably never let me find out who holds such power over you. The wretches can't avoid the charges of murder, I realize that. So just tell me how the bailiff is going to interrogate them, because no one knows their language."

"The court has its methods of finding out the truth," his father said coldly. "Don't you trust their ability?"

"Of course," Henrik replied quietly. "I know that they have their methods of coercing confessions out of people. But the foreigners will understand neither what they're being asked nor what they're confessing to." His voice was rancorous as he continued: "I just thought that the court—and *you*—would place the love of truth above cowardice and revenge."

His father gasped, insulted and furious. "You're talking about two crazy wild animals!" he cried. "Two devils who . . ."

"Father!" Henrik yelled back. "That's not true! And you know it! What are you so afraid of—or who?"

They went on like this all night long. Throwing accusations back and forth at each other, pleading and persuading. When morning came, they were exhausted, but agreed on what to do.

Henrik had told his father about his conversations with the creatures, but not everything he had confided to me. He didn't say a word about his belief that they were descendants of our forefathers. That would have been too much for Master Mowinckel to accept, sheer heresy and madness.

The master was quite proud of his son's abilities, and he was very impressed to hear that Henrik had studied their language. Relieved, he said yes to

Henrik's offer to serve as interpreter during the trial.

Henrik begged his father to do his utmost to see that the High Court did not sentence them to the most severe punishment under the law—death. His father reluctantly agreed. Maybe he thought that, in spite of everything, the wretches were worth more alive than dead.

Master Mowinckel kept his word.

A short while later the bailiff and the councilor came to call.

They sat huddled together in the green parlor, with suspicious glances and stern expressions, while Master Mowinckel spoke eloquently about the Greenland expedition. He described its significance for the honor and fame of the Dano-Norwegian Empire. He spoke of the law of the land and the magnanimity of the High Court, saying that it would serve the glory of God, the King, and the city council if the misdeeds of the deranged creatures were tested before the court, despite the flimsy evidence. Here he slyly introduced the fact that Captain Davis, who had brought the murder charge against the heathens, was known far and wide for his honesty. And yet he had tried to cheat the master out of three barrels of blubber. "But enough of that," Mowinckel went on in a gentle voice. "The most important thing is that justice be done."

In florid phrases he praised the city council's great sagacity, wisdom, and well-known interest in the advancement of the true sciences. He was sure that the city council realized the loss that science would suffer if the rare creatures were to be executed. Finally, he once again lauded the city council's great competence, which naturally enough did not include knowledge of the heathens' unknown language. But now they were so fortunate that the master—in all humility—was able to offer the services of his learned son as interpreter, since his son had studied the language and habits of the wild people for a long time.

The attitude of both the bailiff and the councilor changed during the long speech. The expressions of suspicion gave way to mild interest. The bailiff nodded several times.

"This is wise advice, Master Mowinckel," said the bailiff slowly. "We, the sheriff and the bailiff, are obliged in the name of the Dano-Norwegian crown to enter a charge of manslaughter against the unknown heathens. I understand that you also wish the law to be obeyed. That's good. But I have to ask you if there is any truth to the many rumors in our town concerning witchcraft? The law requires that there must be proof of maleficium when the accusation is made. I know of no such proof—do you?"

It was quiet for a moment, but Master Mowinckel's voice was steady when he replied. "No. I know of no such proof. As the bailiff is aware, the heathens have been locked up and chained in the dungeon at the town hall since they arrived here. How could they have committed witchcraft?"

"Good," said the bailiff, getting to his feet. "Then we know what we can tell Pastor Absalon, who believes that the heathens are practicing maleficium, but without being able to produce witnesses or proof of it."

So it was Pastor Absalon who had threatened the master!

I heard Henrik gasp for breath, just as surprised as I was.

The news about the trial brought both relief and disappointment to the town.

All those who had lived in fear that Satan and all his evil deeds were loose were relieved. Now they could sleep securely in their beds again, for the indictment was for manslaughter and not for witchcraft. Those who wanted a witch trial and burning at the stake as warning, or popular entertainment, were disappointed.

Among the disappointed was Pastor Absalon. He thundered on about devilishness and God's punishment from his pulpit, and he made me nervous.

Henrik consoled me. "He doesn't have a scrap of evidence, Christine! No one has proof or testimony that the poor foreigners have harmed anyone. You yourself know what the sheriff and the bailiff said, that an accusation of witchcraft can't be brought without proof."

"Yes, but Pastor Absalon . . ." I began in despair, but Henrik interrupted: "Don't be afraid of him! The church has nothing to do with witchcraft trials anymore. That was in the old days. Now it's the court that . . ."

He broke off, suddenly aware of my despair. His

hand lightly touched my shoulder. "What is it, Christine? What are you afraid of?"

I tried several times, but the words caught in my throat: "I . . . I . . ."

"You? What do you have to do with . . . ?" Suddenly he understood. "You can be forced to testify . . . But you know that it isn't true! Christine, look at me!"

I couldn't. The tears blinded my eyes, but he could not meet my gaze, either. Maybe he could read something there that I didn't want to tell him—about the unicorn, the strange voice in my head, about the grief over Father and the thirst for revenge that gnawed at me, and about my terrible fear of red-hot tongs, which I knew would make me confess anything—a seething sea of emotions that never left me in peace.

Crying was my only consolation, for both Henrik and I knew that if Pastor Absalon had his way, I would be quite alone in choosing between the foreigners' lives and my own.

"Make way for the High Court!"

The forceful voices of the watchmen cleared the way for the solemn black-clad men, for Master Mowinckel, Henrik, and me.

The streets were teeming with people, happy, excited.

A procession of old and young, drunkards and whores, beggars and peasants, widows and orphans, followed behind us to the town hall and made themselves comfortable on the ramparts in anticipation of a judgment that might be good entertainment.

The day was bright, but for me it was as dark as night.

It was as if I were facing my own trial.

They were sitting close together in the dark, as usual.

It was quiet when we entered the dungeon, but it was obvious that they had been talking to each other.

When the torches lit up the darkness, I met the female's gaze, courageous and challenging.

For the first time since that terrible day when the ship came back without Father, I heard the voice inside me, consoling, kind. And I blushed, happy to know that we were still one, ashamed of the betrayal that cowardice might make me commit.

"Let that never ever happen!" I prayed, and hoped God would listen to a miserable outcast, and not to his servant Pastor Absalon.

The judges shifted uncomfortably, staring in fright at the fur-clad creatures. The loathing shone in their eyes.

"Let me be alone with them, then I can explain to them about the trial," asked Henrik, and the judges didn't have to be asked twice. They couldn't get out of that stinking darkness fast enough, where the shining eyes of the foreigners followed their slightest move.

The cool council chamber filled me with new fear.

The chamber was long, narrow, and dismal, with dark brown timber walls and heavy soot-black beams in the ceiling. The meager light that filtered through the cool green windowpanes lent a strange pale tinge to the judges' faces, like old paper. They waited, silent behind their bare oak table, as their shadows formed pointed black bird wings on the wall.

I shuddered, and felt the cold of the room creep into my body. I slipped onto the bench down by the door, trying to make myself invisible in the dim light. I thought I was alone. Then suddenly I saw Pastor Absalon and Dr. Abraham. My heart leapt with fear and my hands grew clammy.

Would it happen now?

They came in.

Four guards dragged the creatures between them and threw them brutally to the floor in front of the black-clad men. Henrik and his father hurried in behind them.

Henrik wanted to help the creatures to their feet, but he was stopped.

"Let them be!" The sharp voice belonged to the eldest of the judges, a dried-up old man with trembling, claw-like hands.

Henrik obeyed.

The male struggled to his feet and helped the female up.

They waited calmly, with heads held high.

"Make them kneel!" The old man's voice was like ice.

Henrik opened his mouth, but stopped. He whispered something to the creatures, quickly and imploringly. Both shook their heads firmly.

"They prefer to stand," explained Henrik. "It's easier that way . . ."

"I said *on their knees!*" snarled the old man. "Wild animals must be tamed!"

Henrik wanted to protest, but the bailiff broke in: "We are not here to tame wild animals, Your Honor, but to pass a fair judgment. Let the accused remain standing, I say. The court is in session! Read the indictment!"

The trial lasted for many hours.

The creatures stood the whole time in their heavy chains, proud and calm. They answered all the bailiff's questions in that strange musical language of theirs. The male replied most often, but now and then the female would break in with a voice as soft as a spring breeze. I felt the knots of fear loosen.

Henrik was wonderful. Only he and I knew that he and the creatures scarcely understood each other, that the language he used was a mixture of Icelandic, Latin, bits of words and phrases he had learned of their language, and words he made up as he went along. Only he and I knew that they were communicating more with looks, expressions, and hand movements than with words. It was an act—a lie. But a just lie. Even God would have to admit that, I thought timidly.

The creatures had to answer the same questions over and over again: Where do you come from? What is the name of the king of your country? Do you believe in the Almighty, Merciful God? Do you worship false gods? Are all the people in your country heathens?

Why did you attack the ship? Why did you kill the sailors? How? Why? Why? Why?

It went on for many hours, as the light in the room faded and my stomach began to growl from hunger.

The tired faces of the judges shone gray in the evening darkness.

Henrik stood just as straight and calm, listening respectfully to the bailiff's questions, whispering in his odd language to the creatures, and translating their replies, always the same:

Our land is Greenland. We know no king. We know no Almighty God. We do not know any false gods. We did not attack the ship. We intended to trade peaceably with the sailors. We killed no one. They struck us and killed our father and brother. We were captives in the dark.

"They deny everything!" The old man was in a rage.

"Perhaps they're telling the truth," said Henrik cautiously, looking at the bailiff.

"We'll never find out," sighed the bailiff wearily. "This trial must have better proof than what we have heard up to now. Master Mowinckel," he said, suddenly authoritative in his tone, "you have accused these creatures of murder; do you have evidence of which the court is not aware? We have attempted to find the sailors who were aboard the unfortunate ship, but to no avail, and Captain Davis who, hmmmm . . . accused these heathens of murder, sailed to Holland several weeks ago, we understand. Have you anything to say to us?"

I could see from Master Mowinckel's posture that he was deathly afraid. His voice sounded like that of a naughty boy when he replied. "The honored court should know that I was forced to . . . I mean . . . that I saw it as my duty . . ."

"We understand," interrupted the bailiff. "You did your duty as a citizen, Master. But do you have proof that the heathens are murderers?"

"I . . . I . . . Captain Davis accused the heathens before the eyes of hundreds of people . . ." stammered Master Mowinckel.

"Yes," interrupted the bailiff impatiently. "But *proof*, Master. Proof!"

"Captain Davis swore that the heathen female killed sailor Claus Pedersøn," replied Master Mowinckel, almost offended. "But I don't think the heathens should be condemned to death, because . . ."

"It is *we*, the High Court, who shall decide the punishment for the deranged murderers! Not *you*, Master Mowinckel!" shrieked the old man suddenly.

The bailiff cleared his throat. He fixed his eyes on the quivering master. "Allow me to ask you straight out, Master. Do you yourself believe that the heathens are murderers?"

The room fell silent. I felt the cold nipping the skin on my arms.

"I . . . I . . ." began the master.

"Answer Yes or No!" The bailiff's patience was about to break.

"With the permission of the court . . ." Henrik's voice was soft, respectful.

The bailiff listened.

"My honored father would like to use Captain Davis's *logbook* as evidence in this matter. I have only slight knowledge of law and justice," continued Henrik modestly, looking hopefully at the bailiff, "but I know that logbooks have been used as evidence in many cases . . ."

"Because the ship's log is an exact account of all important events on board," interrupted the bailiff. "That is correct. The court requests that you read from the logbook."

There was a great commotion among the judges. The old man was about to burst from anger, and I heard Pastor Absalon and Dr. Abraham hissing excitedly to each other. Master Mowinckel was just as surprised as I was.

Henrik hadn't mentioned a word to either of us. He must have gone in secret to the master's office to get the logbook. So that's what Henrik had been working on, night after night—searching for proof of the creatures' guilt or innocence in the captain's own diary!

"Honored High Court," began Henrik respectfully. "It is unnecessary to read everything from the time the ship left our town until it reached Iceland and later Greenland . . ."

The bailiff nodded.

". . . so I'll begin with the first meeting with the natives of the country."

The room was completely still while Henrik read aloud about the Dutch ship, which entered a large bay in the northwest of the country, there for the first time encountering "the savages," as the captain called them. They came in many small skin boats, surrounded the ship with friendly shouts and gestures. They wanted to trade goods with the ship's crew, and the captain asked them aboard. There, one of "the savages" took an oar, then two of "the savages" were killed and two taken prisoner.

Suddenly one of the judges broke in, a man with a sharp face and wise eyes.

"Why did the captain kill the two natives?" he asked.

"Because they took an oar," replied Henrik. "Shall I read it again?"

"No," answered the judge calmly. "It's not necessary. I just can't understand that the captain would kill two creatures for—for the sake of an oar!"

The other judges murmured loudly, but the old man was furious.

"Continue!" he yelped. "We are supposed to hear about the murder of the sailors, not about the wild heathens!"

I could see that Henrik blanched, but the bailiff said firmly: "Continue!"

And Henrik read slowly on—about how the ship sailed into a new bay. There the crew saw many boats, but none dared come near the ship. After that, the ship was beset by many accidents, illness broke out on board, and they ran into a violent storm which raged for many days. The ship drifted helplessly along the dangerous coast toward the southern tip of the country. There it lay weather-bound in a desolate bay as the hard winter set in. Several of the sailors drowned in the storm, and others fell victim to scurvy and frost-bite. There was no help to be had. One day they saw a ship frozen in the ice far out in the bay. The crew was terror-stricken. They thought that the ship was an omen of their own doom, which caused them to gather all their strength. Thus they managed to sail the ship to Iceland, where it lay at anchor over the winter.

"I do not need to read the rest?" said Henrik, closing the logbook.

"Not as far as I'm concerned," said the judge with the wise eyes, dryly. "I see that there is not one word in the logbook stating that these two accused heathens murdered any of the sailors."

"No," said Henrik calmly. "The accusations are mentioned nowhere by the captain. I have but slight knowledge of law and justice, but it appears that the logbook indicates that *the heathens did not murder any sailors*."

Good, clever Henrik! Now I suddenly realized what he had been doing in such secrecy all by himself. He must have known what rage he would unloose: Master Mowinckel, furious because his son had tricked him; Pastor Absalon, who was cheated out of an ex-ecution he wanted for some horrible reason; the iras-cible old man who wanted to do away with the heathens.

How much wrath you bring upon your head! I thought proudly, and at the same time felt my own conscience burning. I, fearing for my own skin, would have betrayed the foreigners.

"Silence!" thundered the bailiff, and the excited voices hushed.

"Your Honor!" hissed the old man. "The logbook tells us nothing!"

"On the contrary, it tells us a good deal!" replied the man with the wise eyes, sharply. "The uncertainty is now even greater."

He rose, turning to the bailiff and the other judges.

"Good citizens. After what we have heard today, I vote that the uncertainty should benefit the accused creatures. For the sake of our consciences, we cannot condemn them to death, when there is no proof of their complicity in murder. But neither can we set them free; for that the uncertainty is too great. Furthermore, what would the lost heathens do with their freedom? They would no doubt fall in with bad company and end up as criminals."

The loud unrest among the judges forced him to stop talking.

"Are we to believe the lying heathens?" howled the old man.

"The honorable judge is saying only that this court cannot condemn the heathens to death when the proof of their guilt is so slight," said the bailiff firmly. "In that I agree with you, Judge. The young Henrik Mowinckel has shown us that we have only the captain's oral accusations to fall back on. With that, you, Master Mowinckel, have also answered my question, haven't you?" He gazed sternly at the master. "You don't believe that they are guilty after what we have heard?"

Master Mowinckel's "No, I don't believe they

are guilty" was barely audible where I was sitting.

"Good," said the bailiff. "Let the court hear the rest of your proposal, good judge."

The man with the wise eyes was still standing. He seemed relieved, almost happy. "I propose that the court sentence the heathens always to remain in the strict custody of a responsible citizen, such as Master Mowinckel."

In the silence that followed, Master Mowinckel could not manage to keep quiet. "The heathens are . . . *my property!*" he blurted out.

"*Your property?*" The judge's voice was cold as ice. Even in the flickering light of the torches I could see that his eyes shone with contempt. "Do you intend to trade in human beings, Master Mowinckel?"

"They . . . they aren't *human beings* . . . not God's creatures! They're wild . . . like animals!" Master Mowinckel's voice quivered with defensiveness. He stuttered on: "They are *my* share from the Greenland expedition, and I want to sell them—in the name of science!"

His voice was weak in the heavy silence.

"Is it more contemptible than taking black heathens in Africa to the plantations in the West Indies? Many of the shipowners in our town consider that good trade, as several of the judges well know!" he concluded with ill-concealed malice.

I was frightened by the uproar. I never would have believed that grown men could cackle like angry hens!

"Enough!" shouted the bailiff. "That is quite enough! Show respect for the court. Judges, you have heard the proposal. Do you say Yea or Nay?"

A mumbled chorus of "yea," and one piercing voice that howled "Nay!"

The old man was shaking with fury. His thin finger was not pointing at anyone in particular when he hissed: "You'll regret this! We're not finished with these deranged creatures yet, for they haven't been tried for witchcraft and devil worship, have you forgotten that?"

"There is no proof of that!" The bailiff's reply was quite curt.

"Proof?!" cackled the old man. "Ask people in town who live in fear, trembling for their lives! Ask Pastor Absalon, who is sitting in this chamber!"

When the pastor calmly walked forward in all the commotion that followed, I knew that my time had come. Long before he opened his mouth, I knew what he was going to say, and I shook so violently I thought I would fall off the bench. The pastor's silky voice was like an invisible net that tightened around me as he told the bailiff and the judges that I—the poor daughter of the murdered sailor Claus Pedersøn—guarded the heathens every day and knew all their heathen ways and evil deeds better than anyone.

The protective darkness in the corner by the door was suddenly splintered by eyes staring at me. Frightened, surprised, triumphant, beseeching eyes, and I prayed a futile prayer: "God, give me strength!"

Without realizing it, I had stood up and started to walk toward the bare oak table, the accusing men with their sharp bird-wing shadows threatening, flickering in the light.

The bailiff's eyes bored into mine. "Have you anything to tell this court?" he said sternly.

"I don't doubt she has," exclaimed Pastor Absalon.

"Hush, Pastor Absalon," said the bailiff firmly. "Let me remind you that this is a trial for murder, and not witchcraft. But even witchcraft is no concern of the Church nowadays."

"Blasphemy! Desecration of God's holy laws! Is that not a matter for the Church?" Pastor Absalon's voice was anything but silky.

"I agree," said the bailiff wearily. "If the young Christine can tell us that the heathens are practicing maleficium, chained in the dungeon. And if she can tell us that the heathens are mocking God."

Time! I had been given a tiny bit more time to collect my thoughts and my strength. As I opened my mouth to answer, I heard the voice again in my head: "We are one . . . we are one. We share a fate . . ."

I nodded weakly, and said as loud as I could: "No!"

"No?" repeated the bailiff.

I swallowed hard. "No, the heathens do not mock God. No, the heathens don't do anything . . . anything evil to the people in our town." I had to swallow one more time. My throat was as dry as paper when I continued: "No, I don't believe that the heathens murdered my father."

My knees wouldn't hold me up any longer. I sank to the floor and felt the darkness close around me. Far away I heard the old man and Pastor Absalon shouting at each other that people demanded a fair judgment, that they would find some proof, that perhaps I was in league with the devils, that . . .

As the soundless darkness engulfed me, I heard an unrecognizable voice whisper: "You'll regret this, Christine." Then it was too late. I just wanted to fall, fall, fall . . .

Many days later Henrik told me the rest.

The High Court did not condemn the creatures to death for murder, but they were not acquitted either. They were transferred to the custody of Master Mowinckel, with strict orders for them to be immediately examined and interrogated by learned men in science and theology, then Pastor Absalon would exorcise Satan, and the creatures would be entrusted to God's mercy.

Henrik was almost cheerful after the judgment, but I was uneasy. I couldn't forget the voice that promised revenge. The creatures had escaped this time, but the terrible accusation of witchcraft remained, like a bonfire that was not yet lit. Someone would light it, if they could. Then the creatures and I would truly share a fate.

"*I* will."

"You can't."

"I will anyway," he said stubbornly.

Osuqo couldn't see his eyes, only his shiny black forelock, which was just as obstinate as he was.

"Mother and Father have said no. You know that."

Chubby arms were suddenly clasped around her neck. Black eyes stared into hers. Black with glints of gold and laughter.

"Osuqo! You're my best friend."

"You still can't do it."

They were sitting silently in the heather. Little Brother's hand gently brushed over the tiny glowing flowers, part of the brilliant bounty that nature had given the land.

The summer was almost over. The journey back to the winter settlement was about to begin.

"They want me to go with them," he said suddenly.

"You? Little Brother. You're too young!"

"Grandfather and Grandmother want me to go. Grandfather has something to give me when we get there. I *want* to go, Osuqo. Can't you ask Father and Mother for me again?"

"Oh, Little Brother!" Her tears were close at hand now.

She had dreaded this all summer long. Now Little Brother was making it more difficult, but he didn't understand that.

Home at the winter settlement, when they had started out on the long journey to the summer encampment, Osuqo had realized that it would be Grandmother's last journey.

Grandmother had never recovered from the long famine the previous winter when the storms had raged day after day and the hunters couldn't go out on the ice after seals. Without fresh meat, their supply of dried meat and fish had diminished very quickly. Trapped inside the longhouses, the families had to ration their food. But Grandmother had refused to accept even the few scraps that everyone got each day. "It is the young who need energy, let them have it. My strength will soon be gone anyway." Osuqo had seen her give Little Brother most of the small amount she accepted. He had managed better than most during the long famine, but Grandmother had grown thin and weak. When the time came for the summer journey, Father had looked at her anxiously. "I'll manage the journey to the summer encampment," she had said calmly, "but you know it will be my last one." Father had nodded silently, and Osuqo realized with sorrow that her grandmother would choose a different path when summer was over and the deadly winter cold approached.

Osuqo knew very well that the nomadic people had lived with this law of life from time immemorial. She understood that when sickness or age turned the body into a painful burden, the soul had to be set free. Many old people before her grandmother had chosen the narrow path up to the top of the mountain where it split into a jagged cliff that cut right down to the inland lake in the summer land. Her grandmother, too, would choose the leap from the mountain rather than the pain and shame of being a burden to her family.

This was so easy for Osuqo to understand when it concerned other people, but now it was *her* grandmother and she ached with sorrow.

Now her stubborn little brother wanted to accompany them to the ancestral place.

He's too young! she thought, and knew at once that that was a lie. His body was still small, but his thoughts, his mind, and his love were big enough.

Hadn't she herself seen the wonderful friendship that had developed between him and his grandparents that summer? He had grown closer to them, just as she had.

It was as if she saw the old people clearly for the first time when she realized that Grandmother was going to leave them.

Suddenly it was more important than anything else to get to know Grandmother. Hear what she thought and felt, and listen to the tales of her life. Osuqo was near her, gathering, gathering—words, gestures, actions, gathering images that would always be *her* grandmother.

Grandmother had shrunk that summer. She had become dried up and small. Her hands were still beautiful, even though they were ominously thin.

Like delicate brown butterfly wings, thought Osuqo as her grandmother worked with a pair of fine skin pants. No one did such beautiful skin embroidery as she did.

"The pants are for you, my dear one." She smiled. "For your marriage, for it won't be long now, will it?"

Osuqo blushed deeply and felt the tears burning in her eyes. How did she know? Had she seen the looks between her and Poq? Probably. Nothing escaped her sharp gaze. But Poq wouldn't come for her in the longhouse until spring, and then her grandmother wouldn't be among them anymore . . .

"I will never leave you," said her grandmother gently. "You will receive my magic words before I go, remember that. One day you may need them. Then I will be there with you."

Osuqo bowed her head and let the words sink in.

Suddenly Little Brother was there. Pushed past her and put the young swan in Grandmother's lap.

"It won't eat," he said sadly.

It had grown big, had lost its downy feathers. The young swan was beautiful and helpless.

"That's not so strange," said Grandmother dryly. "You feed it too often."

"But it has to eat to grow big and strong so it can fly and be free!"

"Then you must teach it freedom and independence," she said sternly. "Teach it to catch food itself, don't catch food for it."

"But it can't do it alone. It's too young," said Little Brother. "I can."

Grandmother laughed and took his head in her hands. "Stubborn little goat! How would you like it if your father didn't let you manage on your own? Just imagine!"

"I'd be mad!" he exclaimed.

"Exactly. Go to your grandfather, he knows everything about the way swans catch food themselves. Then you can teach the bird freedom!"

It was a strange summer. Like all the others Osuqo could remember, with the same long walks to find puffins, which they stuffed into the skins of newly slaughtered seals and put aside to cure, the same aching back after gathering berries, the same stiff fingers after flensing, tanning, drying, and hanging. The summer days ran on like a peaceful stream, just as warm, just as fine, and utterly different.

The difference was the tension.

That summer was like a taut bow. An arrow quivering at the bowstring, ready for release. There was no way back. Everyone knew it, and it made them extra-sensitive.

Osuqo's mother also changed that summer. Her

stern, reserved mother dissolved in sudden tears and laughter.

The most beautiful thing was seeing her grandparents grow together, their roots intertwining like two plants.

Her grandfather still went out with the hunters, for he was hardy and strong, and the hand that threw the spear was as steady as ever.

But as soon as they returned from the hunt, he would go to Grandmother. They talked very little to each other; they had never talked much. But they would look at each other, and Osuqo knew that they did not see the same things she did. Grandfather had always told many stories, but that summer there were many more. Beautiful, exciting, frightening songs and tales. The family listened and remembered. They knew that he was giving them their inheritance.

Osuqo's father grew uneasy, but Grandfather stopped him. "I know what you want to say, that I'm still strong and could endure many more winters. But you know that I must decide for myself when it's time, and now it has come, my son. She must not go alone."

That was when Little Brother decided to go with them.

Father and Mother said no, but he would not give in.

Soon afterwards Grandfather decided not to go out with the other hunters.

"I have more important things to do," he just said when the hunters tried to persuade him.

The thing that was more important than going with the hunters was building a kayak for Little Brother and teaching him all the secrets of the hunt.

Osuqo watched them, with envy and sorrow.

They had such a good time together, the three of them. Grandmother stitched the kayak while Grandfather made the hunting implements and showed Little Brother how they should be used.

They resembled each other, in a way, young and old at the same time, equally absorbed in one another and in the joy of what they were sharing.

She would see them from far away whenever she returned from her walks in the mountains, see her little brother striving earnestly to throw the hunting line the way his grandfather did. She would hear their laughter when her brother amused them with the polar-bear dance he had made up himself. She knew that she was not the only one who would feel the emptiness when they were gone.

Osuqo had often witnessed sudden death. It was brutal and painful, but this long waiting for the inevitable was even more cruel. As the time for separation approached, their bonds to their grandparents grew stronger. She wished for things to be different, but deep down inside she knew that it couldn't have been any other way.

"Are you sleeping, Osuqo?" The voice of her little brother was reproachful.

"No, I'm not sleeping. I'm just thinking," she whispered, raising her head.

[147

"About what you're going to say to Mother and Father?" he said hopefully. "Oh, do it for me, Osuqo! Do it!"

She nodded faintly. It wouldn't do any good to say no. And besides, it was the right thing to do. She never found out what made her parents change their minds. She didn't have to talk very long with them before they agreed. They had probably also realized how wrong it would be to refuse him the right to go with his grandparents on their last journey. But they wanted Osuqo to go, too, so that they could be sure he would come back safely from the mountain.

They were ready for the journey.

Both of them had dressed up. The large bun on top of Grandmother's head was tight and smooth, decorated with many rows of tiny white shells.

It was chilly in the evening sunshine, and the farewell was brief.

Everything had already been said that summer.

Her grandparents walked ahead, with Little Brother between them. Osuqo hung back. She tried to stretch out the time, put off the irrevocable for a little longer.

Grandmother walked slowly. She could manage only a few steps before she had to catch her breath.

"It's a beautiful evening," said Grandfather calmly. "We have all the time in the world. When you can't go any farther, I will carry you."

Little Brother chattered endlessly, asking question after question about everything between heaven and earth: Why do puffins fly so strangely? What do flies eat? Where does the Moon God really live?

And Grandfather answered, gently and patiently. But his eyes followed Grandmother. Ready to carry her when the journey grew too painful.

They had made it halfway up the steep slope when she remained sitting and could not muster the strength to stand up again. Silently he lifted her and held her close like a little child.

Grief burned inside Osuqo. She wanted to scream: Stop! Don't do it! I love you, and you must not leave me!

But she clenched her teeth and continued on the difficult journey. It was their lives and their choice, and she loved them for that, too.

The sun hung night-red on the horizon when they reached the top of the mountain.

In front of them lay the glittering white expanse of stone, striped with blood-red granite.

It was a short way to the precipice.

This is where the journey ends, thought Osuqo.

Grandfather turned toward them, tall and erect against the evening sky.

"Put me down," whispered Grandmother. "Before we part, you must have our magic words, children."

Grandfather carefully put her down on the stones, and Osuqo put her head in her lap. Grandmother's thin fingers gently stroked her as she gave Osuqo her most secret power. Osuqo opened herself and let the words take hold like seeds. She knew that they would grow within her to a unique power.

"But you will always be with me," she said softly, touching the weary face.

Little Brother was sitting close to Grandfather. His round face was listening gravely.

"You have received my magic words and my best songs," said Grandfather. "Go now, and grow up to be a brave hunter, little bird."

"Now we must part," said Grandmother. "Go now. The last moment is ours alone."

Osuqo took Little Brother's hand. They stood for a moment with bowed heads before they turned and walked away from the precipice, without looking back. On the edge of the steep slope down to the valley and the summer encampment, they stopped, listening anxiously. Everything was quiet behind them.

"Wait, Osuqo, I'll show you something wonderful," said Little Brother.

He lifted the young swan up in his arms, high over his head. Then he opened his hands and the beautiful bird, which had been helpless for so long, spread its wings, fluttered tentatively several times, and suddenly took off.

Like an arrow it shot toward the sky, circled around them, and gave a cry of joy that almost drowned out the sound of something falling into the water far below them.

"I won't!"

"You have to, Osuqo! I can't do it without you. We are one."

"It's wrong! Shameful!"

"It's our only chance. You know what they're planning. You know what they think about us."

"They're evil . . . insane. Nothing we say or do will change their opinion of us! They will only steal even more from us!"

"Not all of them are like that," said Poq. "Henrik and Christine are trying to help."

"Two weak sparrows against hungry ravens!" snapped Osuqo bitterly. "They want to help us—to do what? Do you see anything but hopelessness ahead of you?"

"I see freedom," said Poq with longing. "We must seek all paths to freedom before it's too late."

"Oh, Poq," she said simply.

She would follow him, of course. No matter what it cost.

This was not the first time they sat like this, close together with a wall of hopelessness between them.

That's the way it had been since that long day in the room with the black-clad men. The ones who reminded Osuqo of carrion birds waiting for their prey.

After that day came new carrion birds, often. They were no longer allowed to be in peace in the dark dungeon where they dreamed—together and alone —about a different world.

Every day they were dragged into a naked room where the light had the same color as the ocean. Three foreigners were waiting for them. Two behind a table covered with papers. One of them stern and pale, the other gentle, with a friendly voice. The third man was disgustingly fat, with a red face and bulging eyes. It was the first two who questioned and probed and stripped them of everything. The third man sat motionless. But his hands had a life of their own, sliding slowly across his fat thighs.

Henrik was always there as interpreter. Christine was there, too, like a pale shadow in the cold light.

The questions were always the same—about their country, their people, their family, about animals, hunting, food, about their language, their songs, their games.

They had both answered in the beginning. Poq spoke eagerly and with ease, but Osuqo grew more and more silent.

Then the day came when Osuqo withdrew completely from the foreigners. The guards arrived as usual, dragged them into the cold room. The three were already waiting for them. The man with the gentle voice ordered the guards to remove their chains.

The sudden freedom from the heavy chains rekindled hope in them, which was abruptly extinguished at the next command. Two guards held Poq and her while the other two stripped the clothes off them.

The surprise paralyzed them, and they never managed to resist. Suddenly they were standing there, naked and humiliated. The guards put on the chains again. Osuqo saw Poq shut his eyes in despair and bow his head.

For the first time the foreigners had broken his pride. It made her forget her own degradation for a moment.

Then suddenly she remembered the terror, the blood, and the pain, and she pleaded with her eyes: It must not happen again! Never! Never!

But Henrik turned his face away, ashen, unrecognizable. The pale girl put her hands over her face. Osuqo could see that her shoulders were shaking.

The stern man's face was as if hewn from stone, while the man with the gentle voice quietly circled them. Lifted their arms and legs, touched their hair, peered into their mouths and ears, pinched, looked, and mumbled. Never had she felt so helpless and humiliated.

What did he want? Her terror grew as she felt the foreigner's hands and eyes on her and watched him making strange marks and lines on paper.

Then she heard the sound. At first far away, like an echo of a hideous dream, then close by. The dry rustling of outspread wings and burning eyes engulfed her. Fat body waiting as his fingers danced impatiently on his thighs. Stinging breath as the bird opened his sharp, filthy yellow beak, and she screamed: "No! Please don't! No, no . . . not . . ." The words were lost in a moan.

The gentle foreigner stopped, looked with astonishment at her desperate attempt to cover herself with her chained hands. Laughing, he turned to the others. They nodded. The guards removed the chains and threw their clothes to them again.

"They . . . they robbed us of our bodies!" she stammered.

She and Poq were alone in the darkness again.

He didn't answer.

"Poq! Did you see the drawings they made of our bodies? Disgusting figures covered with strange symbols—perhaps evil, magic words! What are they going to do with the symbols? Make *tupilaqs*, evil beasts that kill? What if they capture our souls the way they've captured our bodies! Poq!"

He gasped: "I don't know, Osuqo. I don't understand either, but I'm just as scared as you are. The foreigners aren't like us. They think and believe and act in a totally different way."

He was silent for a while.

"Their drawings are outrageous, it's true. But I don't believe that they're dangerous. I fear that there is even greater evil in store for us at the hands of the foreigners."

"Are you sure of that?!" she whispered, frightened.

She had only his staccato breathing in reply.

It began with new questions—incomprehensible, meaningless words flung at them like accusations by the foreigner with the stone face.

The small, cold room with its cool green light had changed, hot and brilliantly lit by thin white smoking candles.

His voice thundered in the hot room.

Osuqo felt faint, infinitely tired. What did he want them to understand? She looked at Poq. He was stiff and motionless, as if he had removed himself, off on a journey of his own.

She looked at Henrik. His mouth was tightly closed, his eyes firmly shut, as if he were seeking help in a place where she couldn't reach him.

All she knew was that the foreigner with the stone face was some kind of shaman and he was bellowing at them about the foreigners' gods.

Henrik had tried to explain to Poq and her about the god among the stars and his son. They were goodness. Under the sea dwelled Satan. He was evil. These forces fought for people's souls and eternal life, she understood. But why should it concern her? She and Poq had their own gods.

"Thou shalt have no other gods than me . . . the Almighty God our Father . . . Jesus Christ . . . sin . . . heaven . . . hell . . . Satan and all his works . . ."

The foreign words, the hate-filled voice hammered into Osuqo, day after day. She didn't have strength enough to reply. Finally she no longer lifted her eyes from the floor.

Poq tried to reach her, wanted them to attempt to understand what the foreigner wanted, but she shook her head.

"They say that we have sinned," she said. "But I don't understand . . . don't understand . . . don't want to . . ." She turned away from him in the dark. "Leave me alone, I will find strength in my dreams."

"Don't forsake me!" She knew he spoke from a despair that was deeper than her own.

Their fingers sought each other.

But the hate-filled voice continued, thundered at them the way waves thunder against cliffs, and little

[155

by little Osuqo felt a deep shame and guilt. She didn't know why. She only knew that Poq felt the same way. As waves wear down cliffs, the stern voice wore down their confidence and resistance. Soon they were like bewildered children, meek and voiceless among adults.

As their confusion grew, the foreigner with the stone face became more stern, his eyes more filled with contempt.

Poq begged Henrik for an explanation, but he turned away and said: "Do everything he wants. He holds your lives in his hands!"

Osuqo suddenly saw that his eyes were glistening with tears. He was betraying them and felt ashamed. But he bowed to the power.

The guards came to get them earlier than usual.

The room was full of foreigners. Osuqo recognized the black-clad men, but there were others, too. Foreigners with eyes that shone in the glow of the numerous candles burning in the room. It was suffocatingly hot. A singed smell filled the room. Osuqo felt her body trembling as if from fever. Suddenly she knew that the greatest evil was about to happen.

She and Poq were thrown to their knees in front of the foreigner with the face of stone. He towered over them. In one hand he held the shining stick with the little figure on it. Osuqo recognized the suffering in his face as her own. "The Holy Cross," Henrik had called the stick. She knew that it was the foreigners' strongest amulet.

In his other hand the foreigner held many papers covered with tiny, peculiar symbols. "The Holy Scriptures," Henrik called them. Osuqo stared at them as if bewitched. She knew that the foreigners' strongest magic words were hidden in the symbols.

They were the same symbols that the foreigners had used to capture Poq's and her stories about the land of the People, about their own lives and beliefs. Now they had lost everything to the foreigners' amulets.

Poq had told the foreigners that in the land of the People there were no papers or symbols that would capture words forever. In the land of the People, all songs and tales were preserved by the elders, who passed them on to the young and the children. The young took care of the tales until they grew old themselves, then they were passed on to new children. In this way the stories and songs lived on forever in the land of the People.

The foreigners had listened as Poq spoke, but Osuqo had noticed that the face of stone had grown even harsher.

The foreigner with the gentle voice had shown them how their own language could be captured by the little symbols, and they had watched with astonishment. They had given him many poems and songs; many days later he could repeat the poems to them—with no mistakes. They had thought it was a terrifying and wondrous magic.

Now it was just terrifying.

* * *

The cross flashed, the holy symbols gleamed toward her. It was as if they were alive, crawling toward her from the white paper, wanting to force their way into her. She was numb with terror.

The foreigner's voice had changed, from the thunder that hammered inside her head to a keening, high-pitched tone that made the black-clad men bow their heads and fold their hands.

The evil was approaching, she knew it. It was approaching!

She felt Poq tremble. He, too, knew that it was approaching, that they lay helplessly bound, on their knees in front of the foreigners' god and terrible magic.

"What does it mean? What are they doing to us?" whispered Poq to Henrik. His voice was weak with fear.

"Just do what he tells you!" hissed Henrik. The sweat was running down his pale face.

"What are you doing to us?" Poq barely managed to utter the words.

"Satan and all his works are being driven out of you! All false gods are being chased away! You have renounced heathenism and witchcraft! You will receive the sacrament and be baptized in God's name and find eternal life in His kingdom! Don't you understand yet? It's the only way you can be saved from burning at the stake!" Henrik snapped like a terrified dog.

"What are you doing to us!"

Osuqo realized the awful truth, and she screamed out in horror. The foreigners had robbed her father and her brother of their lives, they had destroyed her life and Poq's, they had tortured them and had captured their stories and lives forever with their magic symbols. Now they were going to force the foreign god on them, a god who did not know mercy or compassion for them.

"No!!" she howled, and saw the flashing cross approaching, inexorably.

They were not going to shut out the Mother of the Sea and the Father of the Moon from Osuqo with their evil magic. Her entire life was dedicated to the mother and father of life and death, just as Poq's life was dedicated to the eternal search for paths to the Realm of the Dead. They knew no other gods! They wished for no other gods!

"We can't!" shouted Poq. His voice was steady, but he was quivering with rage. "Never!"

To touch the amulets of the foreigners would mean eternal imprisonment and perdition. They would forever lose the way to the only freedom they desired— the way to the Realm of the Dead.

The foreigners murmured, filled with horror and revulsion. The man with the face of stone gave orders to the guards. They forced Osuqo's and Poq's heads up, held them in painful grips while the foreigner performed his rituals.

They fought against him, but his power was too great.

Terrified, she felt foreign fingers, hard warmth. Felt the cross, flashing coldness. Felt something dry, soft against her lips. Saw the symbols crawl off the white paper and into her mouth. Then she fainted.

She didn't hear the shouts, didn't see the confusion, didn't notice that she was dragged away.

Everything was drowned in the deafening chaos when the irrevocable happened and she became unclean—forever imprisoned like a fly in a spider's web.

The chaos lasted a long time.

She was drawn into a whirlwind of terror and hatred where she could not see, hear, or grasp anything familiar. Only one thing approached her repeatedly—a vague shape that grabbed at her with big, hairy hands before it vanished in a foaming sea like the chaos within her. Was this the punishment? She received no answer, for the chaos overpowered her, and her body remained motionless on the filthy straw in the dungeon while her eyes stared wide open into the darkness.

No one could help her now.

She didn't want them to.

She was far removed from Henrik and the others who shook her, the man with the gentle voice who forced food and drink into her.

She let it happen. Threw up immediately, anyway.

They spoke with concern about her and Poq. The voices came from another world.

They feared that they would die. Why? Didn't they realize that they had robbed them of everything, everything that was worth living for, even death?

Her body cringed with loathing when the slimy leeches sucked at her neck, her arms, and her thighs, sucked out her blood. The gentle voice spoke calmly to her, but waves of nausea forced up bile in painful thrusts until she fainted again.

It was dark inside and out, but in the darkness was Poq.

She knew his thoughts, his body, his hands, his breathing.

They sought out each other, like half people who don't have a whole life until the gap between them is closed.

"Poq."

"Little Sister. I could not reach you in the chaos."

His fingers stroked her long hair, once soft as down, now stiff and tangled with vomit and sweat.

"You've been wandering." Her voice was hopeful.

His fingers pressed lightly against her cheek.

"Have you . . . do you know . . ." She didn't have the strength to finish her question.

"We are not lost, Osuqo," he said softly. "But I am tired. It was a more difficult journey than I thought was possible. We must get away from here before it's too late."

She knew that he was right. They didn't have much time.

Suddenly the hatred burned inside her again, just as strong and alive.

"They've stolen everything! Everything!" she said. "Our thoughts, our gods, our past. They've captured us with their magic symbols and changed us. Don't you see that we are empty shells?"

"Yes. I finally understand what the foreigners' intentions are. They want to shape us in their own image. They cannot bear that we are different from them. They have to steal, crush, destroy. Do you know that they have also taken away our names and adorned us with their own? You are no longer called Osuqo but Maria. And they call me Peder."

They were silent while their hands and skin spoke.

"A new humiliation awaits us," said Poq suddenly. "Henrik gave me the order from the foreign carrion birds. We will be displayed for people's amusement, like peculiar animals. Henrik begged us to do it voluntarily. It would save our lives, he said."

"No!" she screamed. "Don't you think our lives have cost enough?!"

"Osuqo," he said quietly. "We must escape. It's our only chance."

"*O*nly dreams. It's only *dreams!*"

I repeated to myself.

But it was in dreams that I breathed freely, without fear.

The unicorn with the soft pelt and the beautiful horn was gone now. I didn't miss it any longer, even though it had been painful to see it fade, as a drawing on parchment fades in the sun.

The yearning it had created was more painfully alive than ever, in the deep shadows beneath the trees. In the countryside outside the green forest.

It was beautiful, compelling, with soft plateaus and sharp blue mountains.

It kept luring me farther away from the sunny clearing where the unicorn once had played. I let the longing lead me toward an unknown force. A happiness I knew existed, but had never experienced.

The dreams were a promise of truth and love.

They gave me the strength to withstand reality's nightmare of lies, betrayal, and heartless plans, the

way I had heard them in the dark outside Master Mowinckel's parlor.

In the light summer nights the master, Pastor Absalon, and Dr. Abraham would sit in there. They
talked softly about their plans, but I heard everything
with my ear pressed against the doorjamb.

They talked about the future destiny of the
creatures.

Pastor Absalon praised himself for having driven the
demons out of their bodies and consecrating their
heathen souls to God. Saving them from eternal dam-
nation and turning them into proper human beings,
though not like the rest of us. In his voice I could still
hear the old loathing, and I shuddered. I was quite
convinced that Pastor Absalon wouldn't be satisfied
until the witches' bonfire flamed around them. But he
didn't dare say that. Not yet. Not before there was
proof.

Master Mowinckel spoke eloquently about the creatures' great value to science, but also about their value
to the one who was their lord and master. He who
took upon himself the merciful act of teaching the simple to serve God, their creator, and become the faithful
subjects of the King and the Christian authorities.

These were the master's words, but they didn't have
his former ardor and fire.

My suspicion grew stronger.

While the creatures resisted baptism, in the long
days that followed when their bodies fought *against*
life, I had been watching Master Mowinckel closely.

What was he thinking? Pale and sweating, he followed their struggle. I had heard him mumble about wills that would not let themselves be broken by any means.

I had followed their struggle with great admiration. Never had I seen such unbending pride—even unto death.

But I understood that for the master this was dangerous. He reminded me of a man who owned a barrel of rotten apples with spotless skins, and who wanted to sell the apples as soon as possible to someone else.

And my suspicion was confirmed as I listened to the conversations in the dark. Dr. Abraham was silent, for the most part, while the two others avowed their concern for the creatures' welfare. The first time he opened his mouth, he spoke at length about mercy and responsibility, about an honorable task in the service of God and science, and I felt a chill run down my back.

I remembered his eyes, the way they seemed almost nailed to the female's lovely golden-brown nakedness. I remembered his restless hands.

All at once I realized what the life of the creatures would be like—worse than death.

In the dim parlor the three men came to an agreement. Even though I didn't understand all their convoluted talk, I understood that Master Mowinckel—with the blessing of Pastor Absalon—had presented the creatures to Dr. Abraham.

After the terrible ordeals the creatures had endured, Henrik had withdrawn to the peaceful world of books.

Maybe he found there the same consolation and strength that I found in my dreams. Maybe he thought that all danger had passed. Maybe he just couldn't stand to know anything more.

I understood him so well, but I couldn't, wouldn't, bear all that terrible new knowledge alone, powerless. If only he would try to stop the evil plans.

There was a new, agonizing quarrel between father and son.

"Are you out of your mind, Father?! You want to give the unfortunate foreigners to Dr. Abraham as a part of Sofie's dowry? *Are you intending to give human beings as a wedding present??* It's bad enough that my poor foolish sister is going to be married to that . . . that . . . but that he should have the power over . . . over . . ." His stammering and rage overwhelmed him.

His father shouted: "Watch your mouth, son! My patience with you is almost at an end! From now on, you'll dance to my tune! I've been giving in to your foolish ideas far too long, and all they've brought me is bad luck! Shame, misery, and accusations of maleficium! How long do you think I'll be safe?! You are thoughtless and spoiled! But I've had plans for you for a long time, my fine son!"

He was breathing hard, quivering with indignation. His voice was dark with triumph and threats as he continued: "A few years as a regular seaman on a Dutch trading ship will do you good—no! Don't interrupt me. There you'll soon learn decent manners and the good judgment of a merchant! Life at sea will soon break your pride and all the whims you've learned from those ridiculous books!"

I had grown used to hearing terrible arguments between father and son in the Mowinckel household, but never had I heard an argument end so abruptly. Never had I heard such a silence as that following the master's outburst, and I knew that it had struck Henrik like lightning from a clear blue sky.

I knew that his father was threatening to tear all his dreams to shreds and reduce his future to rubble. If his father carried out his threats, Henrik would have to spend his best years toiling as a sailor in a foreign land, far from his comfortable life and his beloved books. All prospects of studying in the King's city would be ruined. He would have nothing but a position in his father's general store to look forward to.

I hoped that his father's threat would have no effect, but it did. Henrik didn't listen to me anymore, for he had his own rational explanation for why it would be "in the creatures' best interest" to become Dr. Abraham's property.

"You see, Christine," Henrik explained—as if I, of all people, wasn't aware of all the dangers!—"the charge of witchcraft can be raised at any time . . . and you realize how much safer the creatures are as the property of the powerful Dr. Abraham, don't you? When they are displayed at the marketplace on the wedding day as a couple of harmless rarities, people will realize that . . . that . . . Besides, it's not uncommon in other countries to give black and red heathens as wedding gifts, I've read . . ." he concluded uncertainly.

[169

I was speechless with disappointment.

"Dr. Abraham's wealth and power are their best protection from the stake. It is far better protection than my father, a simple shipowner and merchant, can give them. You know that," he said dully. But Henrik didn't even believe his own words.

Protection! I thought in despair. What "protection" would that poor female get from the doctor? The mere thought made me feel sick. But I said no more, for I knew that nothing would do any good.

The troublesome creatures who had been abducted from their own land and had met nothing but humiliation and hatred in our town were now losing their last defender. The honest and good-natured Henrik had placed his own security before their fate.

I saw that he was suffering. I sympathized with him. But nothing compared to the sympathy I felt for the foreigners.

When Miss Sofie became engaged to Dr. Abraham at Eastertime, it was celebrated with pomp and splendor. Since then, everyone in the house had been working on the wedding preparations, for the maiden had demanded that it be more splendid than any fairy tale. The doctor had been adamant that the wedding take place soon after the engagement, for he wanted to get the maiden into the bridal bed—with a party that no one had ever seen the likes of.

Now the wedding was only two weeks away, and everyone worked hard to get everything ready in time.

It was to be a real old-fashioned wedding, lavish and

sumptuous. Miss Sofie was to ride in a bridal carriage, and a large, fine procession would accompany her to the marketplace, where the wedding gifts would be displayed for everyone to see. After that, they would be married, and then the procession would continue to the handsome estate of the doctor, where the wedding would be celebrated for several days.

Madame Mowinckel and Sofie were beside themselves with joy. They couldn't get enough splendor and finery. But the master was uneasy. He grew even more troubled when the doctor demanded that his bride wear the old-fashioned crown of Mary that belonged to his family. The master was afraid that the crown of Mary would arouse Pastor Absalon's displeasure, for wearing a bridal crown was an old Catholic custom.

"Luther's teaching requires that we follow the path of truth and modesty," he said meekly.

"Are you calling me a heretic?" snarled the doctor.

"No! No . . . by no means!" the master assured him. He didn't want to get on the bad side of his powerful son-in-law, either.

"Good. You may have forgotten for a moment that I am a God-fearing man who enjoys the great respect of the Church. Both pastors and bishops are indebted to me."

His words were ambiguous, but I had heard rumors in town that both bailiffs and clergymen for miles around borrowed diligently from the doctor.

The master already had enough worries. He had to ride far and wide to invite people to the wedding. He had to borrow horses for the bridal procession, because he had only two skinny carriage horses in his stall, and the bride, her mother, and all the matrons had to have fine horses, the doctor had decided. He had to borrow a bridal carriage, chests for the dowry, woven tapestries for decoration, and, most difficult of all—gold and silver for the bride's bodice.

In the Catholic days, it was the Church that lent out the bridal finery. Since the Reformation, that was no longer allowed, nor did Pastor Absalon appreciate it if the bride's earthly glory in silver and gold outshone God's heavenly glory in His own House.

The master truly had no easy time of it, constantly traveling while serving two masters at once.

But his worries were small compared to mine, I thought.

No one had ever seen the likes of this demanding bride! Every day she devised new work for the women in the house. We spun, wove, embroidered, and sewed the whole day long. We made linen and sheets, covers and blankets—and the wedding dress.

It had to surpass anything the townspeople had ever seen, she demanded. And it was beautiful. Sewn of heavy, deep-red English cloth, gathered at the waist by a broad belt of beautiful gilded roses and heavy Hungarian gold florins.

The bodice was so heavy with silver and gold jewelry that I doubted whether the delicate Miss Sofie would be able to wear it for an entire day. But I knew her vanity, of course, and was sure that she would find the strength somewhere.

As if this wasn't enough, Miss Sofie suddenly decided that she needed three gowns for the banquet. And we sewed—one of amber-yellow silk, one of fine black fabric, and one of green velvet. We had neither the energy nor the time, but the maiden was merciless. She was probably aware that the rich doctor was not generous. The dresses she took with her from her father's house would probably have to last her the rest of her life—if she didn't get too fat for them, I thought rancorously. With no regrets.

For, as we slaved, Miss Sofie sat in the parlor fiddling with what was supposed to be a lavishly embroidered linen shirt for her bridegroom. The work proceeded with infinite slowness, for Miss Sofie kept pricking herself in the fingers. She also got a backache and a headache, she cried. At last her work ceased altogether.

Madame Mowinckel became more maliciously furious than ever, out of fear that the shirt wouldn't be finished in time, or that her darling plump pink daughter would arrive pale and exhausted at her own wedding.

It was my imperturbable mother who had drawn the beautiful rose pattern on the shirt. And she was the one who now took it from the weeping maiden and worked into the early hours of the morning by the hearth to finish it.

I lay in my bed-closet watching her. Wide awake from toil and resentment. Uneasy for the poor foreigners, whom I saw for only a few minutes each day.

No one cared about them anymore, now that they were no longer a threat.

It was painful to see them. See their eyes light up when I came in.

I was ashamed, because they didn't know about the cruel bargain the master had made, because I was relieved to escape from their inquisitive gaze without lying.

And I realized that I missed them. Missed them, really! These two who reminded me so much of my father's death, whom I had hated to stand guard over, whom I had been so afraid of betraying.

I still didn't understand completely, but I knew that it was true that we shared a common fate.

"I've visited the foreigners." Henrik had suddenly appeared and told me what I had been hoping to hear for so long.

"Did you tell them everything, about . . ." I blurted out.

"Of course!" he interrupted me, insulted. "Almost everything," he went on, scarcely audible.

"What do you mean . . . almost?" I was scared.

"You don't have anything to do with . . ." he snapped, and caught himself.

I waited.

"I told them about the wedding procession and about the marketplace. That they were going to be put on display and that they have to show off their skills with spear, bow and arrow, and boats. But . . ."

"You didn't say that they would soon be the doctor's property," I said softly.

He shook his head. "I couldn't do it."

I looked at him for a long time, struggling not to

say anything I would regret. It *was* a shame about Henrik. Fear had forced him to comply with his father's plans, but the betrayal was tormenting him. I knew that.

"So you also understand what is in store for those unfortunate creatures," I said as calmly as I could.

He swallowed heavily. "Do you think I can forget the doctor's lustful look so easily . . ."

"Go on!" The terror lay like ice in my stomach. "Do you know more, Henrik?"

"Yes, something that . . . that . . ." He swallowed again, as if he felt sick. "Something I h-h-heard when I was l-l-listening to a conversation between Dr. A-a-abraham and the learned Mr. Olearius, you know, the one who e-e-examined . . ."

Henrik got no further.

". . . them slowly and shamefully!" I added sharply.

The rest was scarcely audible: "Dr. A-a-abraham promised to have the male killed soon, and s-s-sell the body to Olearius, who w-w-wants to b-b-boil it and d-d-display the skeleton at universities on the Continent . . . for they s-s-say that it will be a s-s-scientific tri-i-i . . ." It sounded like Henrik was being choked by his own gruesome words.

I couldn't comprehend it.

That people could be so calculatingly heartless!

Never! They would *never* be allowed to do anything so monstrous! Henrik and I had to ruin their plans, even if we had to . . .

"I know what you're thinking," he gasped shamefully. "But it wasn't so easy . . ."

"Easy?! For whom!" I almost shrieked.

He winced.

"You can't live with that on your conscience!"

All at once he pulled himself together, dried his tears, and almost snapped back: "Good God! You really think I'm terrible, don't you? Do you really think that I . . . that she will wind up being a victim of the doctor's repulsive lust . . . and we know he will abuse her until she dies, or do you believe . . . do you believe I would stand still and let . . . them b-b-boil . . . that he would become the plaything of scholars and students all over Europe, that . . ." He couldn't go on.

"No, Henrik. I didn't think that badly of you," I said with regret. "Just tell me what we can do."

"Help them escape," he said, suddenly calm. "I know now that the foreigners can never ever live safely in our world. They would always be persecuted, suspected, or abused. They will never learn anything from us but hatred and betrayal. There's no other way out. They have to escape. It just has to be arranged so that Father . . . so that I . . ."

". . . will not be punished," I could have said, but wisely held my tongue. The blush of shame was already burning deep enough on his cheeks.

"I can help," I said aloud.

"You, Christine? No, it might be dangerous for you . . ."

"I want to," I replied bravely, far more bravely than I felt. "You're not forgetting that I'm still their guard, are you? The one who feeds them every day, the one who is going to be chained to them during the bridal procession through town. The one who has to guard them during the party afterwards. All this your father and the doctor have decided. Believe me, I'm probably part of the dowry to the doctor, too. I'll probably go along as part of the load—the faithful servant and guard."

"Christine . . ." Henrik protested unhappily. But I paid no attention to him. No one knew better than I what an uncertain future I had.

"How can I be punished?" I said scornfully. "I, the lowest of the low. The one who has nothing to lose, who has no future, not even a little hope of a secure marriage. I can risk it—I've got nothing to lose."

He said no more, but I saw admiration in his eyes. For a brief moment I enjoyed what would surely be the only thanks I would ever get.

A poor consolation for my courage, and my heart beat faster. I knew that it wasn't just from fear, but also from the joy of serving the truth, the way I knew it from my dreams.

Henrik made plans alone, for my days and nights were bursting with work for Miss Sofie.

He visited the foreigners often now, and talked to them about the escape plans. We had agreed that they mustn't be told about the doctor's most evil plans. Those were too cruel to torment them with. Besides, we were both afraid that the proud strangers would rather take their own lives than play our game for freedom if they found out.

I was in a dark passage with no light, crawling slowly like a blind larva between the town hall, the house, the weavers, the glove makers, the button makers, and the dry-goods shops—always late, always with new burdens awaiting me.

Now it was tapestries and a canopy for the bridal bed, tablecloths and bench rugs the gracious maiden wanted. The matrons—her bridesmaids—had trudged all over town borrowing all this finery from the rich merchants, but Sofie had set her mind on *owning* most of it. She yapped and wept so long that her father and mother gave in, and we in the household took on new burdens. As did the widows of the sailors who died on the Greenland expedition.

Henrik stopped me once in a while on my hurried trips between the parlor and the kitchen. He quickly whispered his plans, and I glimpsed some light in the dense darkness.

The foreigners and I had to act compliant and amenable. I had to promise not to reveal by any expression how disgusting I thought the whole thing was.

I promised, and Henrik told me the idea he had planted in his vain sister, which she had immediately conveyed to the doctor as an honorable and pious wish.

It would be an even finer wedding banquet—Henrik had said—if the creatures, who were also her property, were dressed as bride and bridegroom and married at the reception. This was an almost forgotten custom to which she—Sofie—could lend new life, and which would surely amuse the guests. Henrik knew his sister's loathing for the foreigners she had never seen. Sofie had thought about it thoroughly for a long time.

Finally she said yes. It would amuse the guests more than dancing bears or jugglers. But the creatures had to wear simple clothes.

But of course! The self-centered Sofie was probably afraid that some of the splendor might be stolen from her own gold-encrusted, pudgy beauty—even by two prisoners.

Mother and I had the sad task of decorating them for the humiliating farce.

Mother had not seen them since the unhappy day when the ship returned without Father.

When the rumors were seething that the creatures had murdered Father, that they were Satan's helpers, she hadn't uttered a word. And she didn't after the trial, either.

It was as though they didn't exist in her world, where only the memories of Father and the dream of the refuge at the mouth of the fjord were alive.

But when she stood in the dark dungeon, which stank worse than ever, she exclaimed: "This is shameful!"

Sympathy aroused her interest, and she marched angrily out to the guards. I remained behind, uncertain, staring at the flickering shadows of the foreigners in the weak light, listening to Mother's authoritative voice. Then she came right back, and behind her came the guards with brooms and more torches.

In the brilliant light the misery became quite apparent.

The walls were slimy with filth and mold. The floor

was one big mud puddle, which even the rats avoided. The straw that had once served as their bed was spread all over, disgustingly black and alive with lice and other vermin. They had managed to keep one corner free of garbage and filth. There they sat close together, as if on a little island, and stared at us intently. Prouder than ever.

"Get moving, child!" Mother said curtly, sticking a broom in my hands. "Sweep it all out. It's crawling with . . . ugh! No decent person would make even the most miserable beast live like this!"

I trembled in fear. It had been a long time since I had seen my mother angry. She couldn't think . . .

"Don't worry, child," she said calmly. "You're not to blame for this. You just work for Master Mowinckel and his powerful friends. But hurry, let's show the foreigners that there is some mercy in our town!"

While Mother and I swept out all the filth, the guards brought in a wooden bathtub, brushes, and clean rags, and finally some new straw.

The foreigners watched attentively, without the slightest sign of uneasiness.

They trusted Mother, I could feel. It struck me that she was the first grown woman they had met since they were captured. She was determined, but kind, and they did everything she wished, without a word passing between them. It was as though they finally had found a friend.

Mother asked the guards to remove the chains so they could bathe. Then she sent out the guards. They protested at first, saying that the creatures were dangerous wild animals, but Mother just snorted and shoved them out.

The foreigners undressed quickly and without shyness.

Mother inspected their fur clothing with a wrinkled brow.

"Frightful! It's a wonder they aren't sick! They've probably had the same clothes on since they were captured. No doubt they were handsome clothes once, according to their taste, but now . . . ugh! That poor girl's trousers are full of dried blood! I wonder what evil fate befell her . . . Now! Don't hang your head, child! Take these clothes out in the fresh air and beat them as hard as you can! The foreigners have dignity. They ought to be spared from amusing people at the marketplace covered in filth and shit!"

With my arms full of stiff skins teeming with lice, I stumbled out into the sunshine. Relieved, ashamed, and happy.

My stern, sweet mother!

So good that she came, fearless and just, as always.

Dignity! I thought, and pounded away at the clothes with the biggest stick of firewood I could find. If there was something that Mother had known how to preserve through all *our* misfortunes, it was precisely our dignity.

So like her to consider the dignity of others.

I hadn't seen their clothes so closely before. I was amazed at how painstakingly they were made. The skin of the long shirts had once been soft and shiny, of the finest quality. Now it bore nasty stains from all the misery the foreigners had been through. I brushed and brushed to get the fur shiny again, while I admired the edge trimmings on the suits, made of hair-fine braided skin.

There was scarcely a furrier in our town who could display such beautiful work, I thought. And there was probably no shoemaker who could make such soft boots, with seams as tight as these.

I had to giggle as I carried the clothing back down to the dungeon. There would probably have been quite a stir if the guildmasters of the furriers and shoemakers had heard a poor servant girl say something like that!

The dungeon smelled almost clean.

Mother was kneeling in front of the foreigners. She was combing the female's long hair with gentle movements. The hair gleamed gold and blue in the torchlight.

I gasped. So beautiful!

The male was finished. His shiny black hair flowed over his shoulders.

I noticed at once the trust between them. It was a closeness, like that between mother, daughter, and son. Henrik and I had never experienced anything like this, I thought with a pang of envy, and caught myself at once. I had never treated them as Mother did either, as *fellow human beings*. The way they sat, calm, content, I saw for the first time a young man and a young woman, only a little older than I was. No longer *crea-*

tures, but foreign people, different from the people I was used to. Suddenly I wanted to know much, much more about them.

I hadn't thought that way before.

I didn't even know their real names, although they had repeated them for Henrik and me and all the accusers—time after time.

Now I sincerely wished that I remembered their names, for I couldn't call them Peder and Maria. That would have been too cruel.

He turned and looked at me.

His gaze pierced right into my dreams.

I heard the wind singing, saw the mist part and reveal the mysterious land. Blinding-white spires high above dark blue halls, supported by huge, green-shimmering pillars. I saw in the heart of my longings.

Or were they his longings?

I held my breath, for a long time, without getting an answer.

The happiness, the confusion made me dizzy. I was about to fall. Almost humbly I handed him the clothes.

"Look at that," said Mother dryly. "You've done good work, my child."

Both of them looked at me gratefully, and I felt hot and dizzy again.

They dressed themselves quickly.

He took out the little skin pouch that was concealed under his suit. She carried a similar pouch. I had seen them when I pounded the clothes, but despite my curiosity I hadn't dared to open the mysterious pouches. I had a feeling that they contained something extremely valuable to them both.

From the pouch he took jewelry, fine leather thongs decorated with shells. He fastened the jewelry around his forehead and by his ears, so that his hair was gathered in thick tassels.

He looked at my mother expectantly.

She nodded solemnly with a satisfied gleam in her eye.

I knew she was seeing the same thing I was—a handsome, proud prince from a foreign land, whom we would never get to know.

"To God, all his children are equal. His mercy and love are just as great toward the poor as toward the rich, toward the insignificant as well as the great, toward the familiar as well as the unfamiliar," she murmured.

For the first time I rejoiced in her deep love of God, for she was the only one—of all the God-fearing people who had surrounded the foreign man and woman—who had been merciful. My simple mother, who could neither read like the scholars nor had power like the merchants, was wiser than they were.

I had never confided my dreams to her. Now I regretted it. It was too late now. The dreams had grown into me the way a tree grows into a wall. I no longer knew how I could explain them.

Suddenly I grew sorrowful. She would never be able to share my longing and joy. But she had her own.

The young woman was painstakingly gathering her hair in a large knot on top of her head. But the narrow strands of the beautiful shell ornament would not contain her heavy hair.

She looked unhappily at him.

He smiled, gently teasing. Stroked her cheek lightly.

She tossed her head. Her hair billowed down her back. Shiny black against the dull white shells, tiny as pearls.

The beautiful ornament that could not hold her hair she gave to Mother. There was a smile in her solemn eyes.

Mother accepted it and smiled back. Warmly, in a way I couldn't remember her having done since Father was alive.

He approached the light, slowly.

The jewelry rattled softly. His body weaved slowly.

The song began, low,
reached through the barriers of fear
and into the dreams
and I heard the wind whistle through the mountaintops,
saw the sea struggle with the land that had erupted
*   from it,*
saw the eagle's eye reflect the glittering prey in the waves,
and her voice rose. Soft, alluring,
and I saw red sun cleave blue-black night
and the sky flame in colors.

I did not dare cry.

Mother sat still, with eyes closed.

Finally she said: "My God is with you. He will never

leave you. And you will always be in my heart, children."

She stood up. They gazed at each other for a long time, and I felt excluded.

We were almost home when I finally dared to ask.

Mother thought carefully before she answered: "My God will look on them with mercy, for their misfortunes are far from ended.

"There is little we can do to spare them, for they must decide for themselves how they are to escape from our chains. Whatever they have done and whatever they will do, you must always remember that their sins are small compared to the sins of those who forced them to come here. Only to end as the playthings of a spoiled girl and her lustful husband."

We walked on in silence.

Whatever they had done . . . Was it Father's death she was talking about? The murder we would never know anything definite about? Of course. It was just like Mother to say so much in so few words.

"Make peace with yourself," she said. As if she knew that the uncertainty about Father's death was plaguing me, that I was still searching for someone to blame. "I have prayed to our merciful God to forgive them. You must do the same, child. They need prayers more than despair and tears."

I nodded in silence.

"You and I must dress them for the amusement of the guests at Miss Sofie's wedding. She would probably prefer to see them in sackcloth and ashes, or dressed up like clowns, but we won't let her have her way, will we?"

I nodded again and felt myself blushing from shame and happiness.

Ashamed of everything I hadn't done, happy about what Mother and I were planning to do together.

"We'll dress them beautifully, but without arousing Miss Sofie's wrath," said Mother decisively.

Now we were sitting together on the edge of the hearth, sharing the meager light and the long hours of work. We scarcely spoke, for we shared the same thoughts as we cut the rough canvas that was to be the feast costume of the young man and woman. The same joy at seeing the simple clothing transformed into meadows full of daisies, larkspur, and anemones, so pale and fine that you had to hold the cloth up to the light to see them.

We were happy as we worked, happier together than we had been in many years.

I wished that it would never end.

But it had to end, for the wedding day was drawing closer and closer. The hours were oddly short on that last night. When morning came, our joy sank like water into sand.

Then we both knew that we had found and lost something forever.

"*I*t's coming! It's back again!"

Osuqo hurried outside with the others.

It was late winter and biting cold. The sun had long since risen after its lengthy winter hibernation, but its rays were cool, without strength now beneath the blue-black thunderclouds.

She saw it immediately, sharply yellowish-white against the gray-green ice.

It was truly a mighty bear. Perhaps it was an enchanted bear, as her brother Kavdeq claimed. Then it would have the same magic power and knowledge as people did.

Its body was enormous. Thin after the winter, but still so heavy that it seemed as if the powerful shoulders and paws supported it with difficulty. Its head was long and wide, yellowish-white like the rest of the beautiful fur, but with a definite white spot on its forehead. It was beautifully shaped, almost like a piece of jewelry. It shone with the same glow as the shells used for ornaments. Osuqo knew that, more than any other animal, the polar bear demanded respect from the people who hunted it, and an enchanted bear demanded the greatest reverence of all.

If it was killed in a humiliating way or the hunters neglected to observe the strict rituals of death, its injured soul might plague the settlement for years.

Osuqo noticed that the bear was restless, as if it was searching for something.

She didn't doubt for a moment that it knew they were there even though it couldn't smell them from such a distance. The bear had been keeping an eye on them for some time. It had visited the settlement many times. Once it had stolen a newly slaughtered seal, and several times it had thrown itself against the house walls, as if to challenge the hunters.

When the hunters stormed out with their spears raised, the bear was gone. As if dissolved by wind and sleet. But its tracks were easy to recognize—a deep trail, with the right forepaw turned strangely inward. Osuqo was certain that it was an enchanted bear and that it wanted something from them. It probably knew that the hour of its death was approaching. Perhaps it feared a humiliating and slow death as the prey of other bears. Perhaps Kavdeq was right and the bear was seeking a slayer, a hunter who could take its life in a battle of equals.

Osuqo looked up at the sky.

The clouds were rounded and black like soot-covered oil lamps.

A bad omen for a bear hunt.

"A storm's coming," said Father uneasily. "It's not a good day for hunting an enchanted bear."

"It is a good day," said Kavdeq emphatically.

"I'll say it again, Father. The time is ripe. Our spears are sharp. The enchanted bear is waiting for us, and we've been waiting for it a long time."

"You're just impatient, son," said his father dryly. "Your eagerness makes you forget caution and good sense."

"Courage is often the prisoner of good sense!" Osuqo's brother replied sharply, and she was shocked by his disrespectful speech. "You know that I'm a great hunter, Father, with a power unmatched by anyone. You know that I've been waiting a long time for the enchanted bear, for it has chosen me to take its life in a worthy battle. *I* am the one who will honor its soul and secure it a speedy road to the Realm of the Dead."

Both his voice and his attitude were arrogant.

Neither Father nor the other hunters said anything after that. But the looks they exchanged should have made her brother blush with shame, thought Osuqo angrily.

He had been intolerably arrogant for a long time, ever since it became apparent to everyone that he had had quite unusual luck in the hunt.

Kavdeq merely had to sit down next to a breathing hole on the ice and immediately the nose of a seal would stick up. While he dragged home one seal after another, the other hunters might wait days by the breathing holes without seeing any trace of a seal.

His luck had made him cocky, but it wasn't until after he killed the enormous old walrus single-handedly that he began his tiresome boasting.

"I'm blessed by the gods!" he shouted, repeating it so often that Osuqo felt like stuffing his mouth with dry grass.

In this way he had convinced himself that the mighty, lonely enchanted bear had chosen him to take its life.

In the beginning Father had criticized her brother's bragging. He had warned him against arrogance, for the Sea Woman might punish the whole settlement for it. But Kavdeq wouldn't listen to his father, and his luck in the hunt continued.

And so Father's criticism ceased because Kavdeq gave his family an abundance of meat and skins throughout the winter, and that gave Father plenty of valuable things to trade with the foreign ships when they came.

Osuqo was uneasy. She was afraid not only that her brother's luck in the hunt would run out but also that his boasting and luck would create bad blood among the families of the settlement. Osuqo had heard about unfortunate blood feuds and poisonous enmity that lasted for years. It could be just as catastrophic for the people at the settlement as lengthy storms, illness, or hunger. Arrogance and envy could take just as many lives, and for years they could hold the people captive in an evil circle of sorrow, pain, and the thirst for revenge.

Osuqo was afraid that this might happen to them,

for she knew of *one person* who was suffering because of her brother's arrogant boasting. That was Poq.

Poq and Kavdeq had grown up together like twin brothers, so devoted and loyal to each other that Osuqo had been envious of them more than once. Silently she had wished that something would break their annoying solidarity.

Now she regretted every little envious thought, for the bonds between Poq and Kavdeq had been broken.

"We're ready," said Kavdeq curtly.

The hunters had gathered outside the longhouse, dressed warmly for the hunt. They were all wearing anoraks and pants made of polar-bear skin, and some of them had put on one or two furs underneath. It was good protection against the biting wind which warned that the storm was not far away, and extra protection against the polar bear's enormous paws and knife-sharp claws.

Poq took the lead next to Kavdeq. His face was expressionless, strange. Osuqo was afraid.

This was a terribly bad day for a bear hunt! A day full of bad omens. The storm, the enmity between the two friends, the uneasiness and reluctance of the older hunters, and the prey with the magic powers.

The women, who usually joked and laughed with the hunters before they set out, were silent and still. Only Osuqo's mother tried to say something, but Kavdeq stopped her.

"No, Mother!" he exclaimed haughtily. "Today you will not give us magic songs that will weaken the bear's strength and reason, for today man and bear will meet in a battle of equals. Save your songs for the fainthearted. I will kill the bear and bring its head home to you!"

Mother bowed her head, blushing with shame. She knew that the arrogant words had struck everyone.

The hunters set out, silent and grim.

In front walked Kavdeq and Poq, hostile and eager for battle. Right behind them came Osuqo's father and the two other hunters.

Osuqo wished deeply that they hadn't left like that, split by the bad feelings. They were heading for misfortune, she was sure of it. She just didn't know whom it would strike.

Osuqo followed them with her eyes as long as possible.

The enchanted bear bounded in front of them. Leading them farther and farther out on the deceptive ice. Always beyond the spears' range, but never so far away that the hunters lost sight of it. The enchanted bear was playing with them, egging them on, provoking ever greater animosity between the two young hunters.

She waited for them all day long.

It was terribly cold to sit still, but the cold inside of her was even worse. Only Little Brother kept her company.

He crept up suddenly and settled himself comfortably in her arms. He sat that way, silently, the whole day.

196]

For once he hadn't begged to go along on the bear hunt. Perhaps the enchanted bear had frightened him, or perhaps it was the ominous mood among the hunters.

The small boy who always had a thousand questions on his tongue was silent. Once in a while he would press closer to her, as if to assure her that he was waiting just as desperately as she was.

Osuqo's eyes ached from staring vigilantly from the ice up to the threatening sky. The violent storm was brewing, but did not break loose.

Osuqo used all her powers to hold it back. If she just sat there like that, pinning the storm down with her gaze and her thoughts, she would be able to spare the hunters one of many dangers, she thought.

The weak spring sun grew smaller and redder in the sky.

One by one, other hunters returned to the settlement, those who had gone out after seal or fish that day. They came back empty-handed and silent. The sea was as if emptied of life.

As if all the animals had gathered at the site where the great battle would take place between man and beast.

The sun was just a blood-red stripe between the sky and the horizon, and the air stood still with the cold.

The people at the settlement were frozen in that long moment which was disconnected from all time, the moment when the hunters would come into view or when they realized that the hunters would never come back.

It was now or never.

Osuqo felt nauseated and exhausted.

Then she saw it.

In the last rays of the sun, something appeared from behind a rounded hill of ice. At first she saw only an odd blood-colored shape moving very slowly toward them. She grew cold with fear. Was it the horrible magic snake, the one that crept through the stories, the one that lived on human flesh alone?

Soon she was able to distinguish five people. Two were dragging someone between them, and two were dragging the bear. It was a horrible sight. They were all so soaked with blood that they were unrecognizable. Slowly they stumbled closer, with a lurching red trail behind them.

Osuqo's mother and the other women wept quietly as they prepared to receive the injured.

The men ran down to the polar-bear hunters to help them home.

Osuqo and Little Brother sat motionless as before. Her eyes did not waver for a second from the sky. The thunder rumbled, like a rock slide down a steep scree slope. The storm was ready to break loose with its terrible, accumulated force.

"Just a little longer!" she pleaded. "Wait—then you can release all your spirits and powers!"

A violent clap of thunder was the reply.

When the bloody procession reached the edge of the shore, Osuqo couldn't stand it anymore. She grabbed her little brother's hand and raced down the slope.

She caught a glimpse of the bloody mass which early that morning had been her proud brother. Then the storm broke loose. The heavens opened. Rain and sleet whipped down.

No one had time to weep anymore. Now it was a matter of getting everyone and everything inside.

She saw Little Brother running along next to the women who were carrying her brother's torn body to the longhouse. Little Brother was holding his lifeless hand. In this way he accompanied his proud brother home from the hunt.

Osuqo helped the exhausted hunters and the other men to drag the heavy bear carcass up the slope. Behind them climbed Poq.

His face was proud and expressionless, but he was carrying the bloody bear head in his arms.

It was a terrible night.

Not until early in the morning were the wounds of the hunters cared for and the bear quartered. Weary and afraid, everyone stood around Kavdeq.

Osuqo felt the nausea rise up inside her at the sight of his mutilated face, especially now that she realized her brother would always look like a monster—if he lived.

He was unconscious when the women placed him on the bed. One of his eyes had been torn out by the heavy bear paw. The other was closed while his mother stopped the blood, cleaned his wounds, and put healing plants on them.

[199

The shaman Aua prepared himself to journey to the Sea Woman to beg for Kavdeq's life.

In the meantime Poq worked to set the enchanted bear's soul free from its dead body. Poq carried out the rituals, silent and somber. Without the joy that normally filled the hunter who had felled a bear.

He placed the bear's head outside the longhouse, with its snout turned toward the Realm of the Dead. On the shining white spot of its forehead he placed his sharpest arrowhead and his best knife. He filled the bear's enormous jaws with fish oil, its nostrils with dry grass, and its throat, too.

Meticulously, lovingly, Poq made sure that the bear's soul had food and presents for its journey and that its throat was sealed so its blood would not run out on the way from life to the Realm of the Dead.

The storm had spent its powers and the young spring sun had risen on the horizon when Osuqo's father gathered them to tell of the bear hunt. This was his tale:

The enchanted bear was truly as clever as a human being! It was also much bigger than we thought. The bear led us farther and farther away from the safe ice near shore and closer and closer to the open water. There the ice had broken up in great floes, and the channels of water between them were hidden in many places by treacherous layers of snow. The bear crossed easily from solid ice to drifting ice floes, for it was able to leap an incredibly long distance. No living person could equal that.

Kavdeq, in his arrogance, wanted to attempt the leaps, but we stopped him. We would have had no chance on a drifting ice floe, perhaps on its way out to the open sea.

When we stopped, the enchanted bear stopped at the edge of a narrow channel. It turned and looked at us challengingly, as if saying: "Test your strength against mine—those who dare!"

Then we attacked, but to our horror we saw that our mighty spears bounced right off the bear, yes, they were even thrown right back at us! The bear rose up on his hind legs and snarled at us, baring his teeth.

It made us older hunters hesitate. Maybe this bear was more than an enchanted bear! But that arrogant son of mine lost control, out of rage. With a howl he raced toward the bear, without a spear, armed only with a small knife. He rushed into the mighty embrace of the bear, with the little knife aimed at the animal's heart.

They danced around in a deadly embrace. Blood spurted from the bear's heart, and the heavy paws slashed my son's face to ribbons.

Helplessly we followed the macabre dance. For a long time we couldn't tell what was man and what was bear, their embrace was so tight. We couldn't hear the difference, for both of them were growling furiously.

But suddenly the bear released its iron grip, raised one paw, and gave my son a blow that sent him backwards, knocked unconscious. The bear was just about to devour Kavdeq when Poq rushed forward with his harpoon raised.

The bear fell over backwards in surprise, and into the water. Then the rest of us ran forward with our spears raised. At the same moment Kavdeq came to and gasped that we should kill it while it lay helpless in the water.

But Poq stopped us and said: "We promised to take the bear's life in a fair fight. Do you remember *who* made that promise?"

Poq was right. Besides, we knew that if the bear was killed in the water, it might sink to the bottom, and then no one would enjoy the meat or the beautiful skin.

The bear was lying still in the water, staring at us. Its head was raised and its gaze was deep and black. Its eyes spoke to us clearly. "Let me come up and take my death standing."

We retreated, dragging Kavdeq with us. He had fainted again.

The bear struggled for a long time to get up onto the ice. It was heavy with water and weak from the battle and loss of blood. Finally it stood there, shaking the water out of its thick fur. Then it spun around abruptly. Snarling, it made a great leap toward us. Poq stepped forward, calm, with his harpoon raised. The bear fell over him and the harpoon thrust right into its heart and killed it on the spot.

We pulled the dead bear off Poq. None of us said a word as he stuck his flensing knife into the neck of the bear and cut off its head.

Osuqo listened with awe to the story of the enchanted bear's death. It was a great story, but she knew that it was not over yet.

The days passed and everyone at the settlement was happy. They gorged on bear meat, for Poq shared equally with everyone. No one denied that it was his bear, but Osuqo wondered what her proud brother would say when he was well enough to realize what had happened.

Osuqo helped nurse her brother.

The wounds healed remarkably fast, but he would always wear the fiery red scar from the heavy bear paw, marking him from the roots of his hair down to his chin.

The bear had also put a stop to Kavdeq's luck in the hunt. With only one eye, his good aim was gone forever.

Life at the settlement continued normally again, but there was an oppressive restlessness beneath the peaceful surface.

Osuqo felt it in her stomach. It knotted up at the thought of what Kavdeq might do to her Poq. Would he kill Poq? Start a blood feud that would poison and finally destroy all their lives?

There were many who shared Osuqo's fear.

One day Aua and Poq came to her father, and they talked quietly together for a long time. The two older men wanted to find a peaceful solution. At the same time they had to respect Poq. He had killed the bear, and he felt insulted by Kavdeq's arrogance. In addition, there was the valuable skin. Who had a right to it? The meat had been divided up and eaten, but the head of the bear had to be buried by the bear's true slayer.

Poq was sullen and stubborn in the beginning, but

suddenly he had a change of heart. He spoke of the evil time when his best friend—practically his twin brother—boasted about himself and scorned Poq. Now the enchanted bear had punished Kavdeq. Poq would give the head and skin to Kavdeq to win back his old friendship.

"It's probably not that easy," said Father heavily. "If I know my son, his pride is as hurt as his body. If you, Poq, offer him the bear he could not kill, he will undoubtedly be mortally offended. His luck is gone, but his arrogance probably lives on as strong as ever. It must be removed with cunning."

Aua nodded in agreement, and Poq gave in at once.

"It must be solved with a contest," said Aua, and that's the way it was done.

Poq and Kavdeq would meet in an amicable competition, with songs and dancing to drums.

Osuqo was both relieved and happy.

A catastrophe would be avoided and the whole settlement would witness the competition in which the two opponents would sing improvised songs and dance comical dances to mock each other. That was always exciting and fun.

Everyone could participate as judges. If the two opponents did not take the competition seriously, but danced badly and sang boring songs, the audience would let them know. She knew that Poq and Kavdeq would pride themselves on being as clever, inventive, and mean toward each other as possible in the songs and dances, so that the settlement would choose a worthy victor in the contest over the enchanted bear's skin and head.

But Osuqo also looked forward to the competition's conclusion and the resolution of the enmity between Poq and Kavdeq. Then they could all join in the real fesitivity after the competition, which she knew could last for many days and nights.

Osuqo sat with her brother until he awakened from his long torpor.

She was the one who cautiously told him what had happened on the bear hunt, and she was the one who waited patiently and without crying while he turned his face to the wall and withdrew into himself with grief and rage. She felt terribly sorry for him. As gently as possible she told him about the competition as he fought his feelings.

Finally he gave in and began to practice his dances and songs.

The day of the competition was as radiantly beautiful as only an early-summer day could be. The water was mirror-smooth in the bay, gurgling softly around the drifting icebergs. The site of the competition lay protected by the marsh-covered slopes steaming hot in the sun.

Everyone was up early that morning. Children and adults were filled with anticipation, and carried with them everything they would need for the long celebration. Warm furs to sit on, an abundance of food, and special delicacies that had been saved for some time for just such an occasion. There was whale blubber, dried halibut, and fragrant, freshly dried sprat.

Drums and dance masks were brought out, and the

people adorned themselves with their finest jewelry made of beads and shells.

Kavdeq and Poq were magnificent as they stood amidst a circle of excited spectators. Both had painstakingly brushed their pants until the polar-bear fur gleamed. Both had decorated their naked torsos with jewelry. Slender strings of shells across their breasts and around their upper arms, and both had adorned their long, black hair with shells.

They were full of pride, as they waited there with drums in their hands for the signal to start. Proud and eager.

The bitter hostility which had ruled them for so long had almost disappeared. Now only pain and the eagerness for battle were apparent.

Osuqo was relieved, but she looked at her brother with sympathy.

How thin he had become! The hideous scar from the bear's paw shone angrily in the sun. It made him look more furious than he actually was, for Osuqo knew that deep inside he was glad that the evil strife would be resolved in such an honorable way.

Between them lay the heavy yellowish-white bear skin. The enchanted bear's head was on top of it. It had begun to decay, but it was still beautiful. The eyes were still black and clear, almost as if the bear's soul had not left them.

The songs and dances began calmly, but soon swelled to a wild tempo. The two slung words and notes at each other and moved in a rhythmic game which revealed both their longing and their dislike. It was like following two lightweight balls through the air, quick as lightning or lingeringly precise. They found each other's weak points, and the spectators appreciated the masterful duel.

Laughter rang out when they described each other as children: whimpering and cunning as puppies; as young boys: boisterous and inquisitive as reindeer; and as adults—in the contest for the enchanted bear's magic powers and knowledge.

The laughter stopped. The spectators watched in silent suspense. Before their eyes a struggle was taking place between two friends whom arrogance and envy had kept apart for so long, and who were now singing and dancing out their mutual sorrow and love.

It was an extraordinary, magnificent contest. Osuqo, like everyone else, felt sympathy for both of them. They had been dancing so long and yet they still had more to say to each other, but they were both close to the limit of their strength.

Suddenly she saw her brother stumble, as if all energy were drained out of him. She saw his head bow powerlessly. She heard his song smothered by a deep sigh.

Then Poq jumped over the enchanted bear's skin separating them.

They hugged each other in a tight embrace and sank to their knees with their heads close together.

It was silent for a moment, then the spectators stood up and cheered. The competition was over without a winner or a loser. Reason and love had won over hatred and arrogance.

The peace of the settlement was assured. Now the real celebration could begin.

Unnoticed, Osuqo went up to the bear head.

Cautiously she lifted it in her arms and carried it to the pile of stones that Aua had prepared for a proper burial.

Before she laid it to rest, she looked into the bear's eyes. They were still deep and clear, as if they were staring at something far beyond her reach.

Later she realized that there had been a hint of triumph deep inside. She also realized that it was not her own voice which said that a good soul makes people beautiful.

*M*orning came, clear and mild.

Few had slept in the Mowinckel household that night. No one had had time to follow the pale night into day, as they usually did, both servants and masters. For nothing was as beautiful and full of sweetness as the first tentative nights of summer.

My head was swimming after days and weeks of toil and lack of sleep. My body mechanically carried out everything it was commanded to do, but feelings and thoughts were remote, hidden in a dark grotto. Fear and humiliation could no longer find their way there. Now I was spared from feeling loathing and shame, while the journey continued toward the abyss.

Mother and I put the finishing touches on the wedding clothes for the young foreigners as the morning of the wedding day dawned. I was called at once to Miss Sofie to help the bridesmaids dress her.

She was standing in the middle of the room, wearing only her underwear, when I arrived. Her face was contorted with weeping. Her arms stuck straight out like a doll's. Her body was quivering with hysteria.

It would have taken the patience of angels to charm her, and the bridesmaids had it. They tied knots, laced, fastened, and basted while Miss Sofie sniveled. All at once she swept them aside and rushed to the window. She thought she heard Dr. Abraham's groomsmen. They were supposed to ride into the courtyard three times and ask whether she was ready to be married.

Miss Sofie had been to the window at least twenty times when we heard the horses snorting for the first time, and Dr. Abraham's spokesman bellowed from the courtyard: "Miss Sofie, are you ready?"

"Yes!" she squealed, and her dressing was allowed to continue undisturbed for a while, as the groomsmen, laughing and shouting, partook of the beer that Master Mowinckel offered them.

Miss Sofie's impatience increased after that, and the bridesmaids had their work cut out for them, fastening the heavy silver and gold jewelry on her bodice without pricking her bloody.

The second time, the men came with drums and trumpets, and they drank even more strong beer after Miss Sofie squealed, "Yes!"

Now they got busy down in the courtyard.

The groomsmen were only coming one more time, and then everything had to be ready for the procession.

The bridal dowry was carried out, along with food and drink in great quantities. The carriages were brought out and the horses hitched up. There was an uproar without equal, and the excitement infected the patient bridesmaids, who suddenly couldn't decide how the beautiful crown of Mary should be placed on Miss Sofie's hair. Bickering, with shaking hands, they tugged at both hair and crown. All the while Miss Sofie was crying as if the end of the world were near.

Then Madame Mowinckel sailed in and took charge. She sent me to see if everything was in order with "the wild heathens."

I dashed down the stairs, relieved to get away from the storm brewing in the parlor.

The courtyard was full of carriages, horses, and people. It was an excited, radiant, noisy hubbub: waving flags and banners, drumrolls and rifle salvos, laughter and song, glittering gold and shiny blue. Festively clad and merry, with one exception.

Like a mold-black spot on a brilliant carpet, the cart with the two foreigners stood out in the crowd.

A dirty old freight cart of the kind used to ship dried fish and barrels of cod-liver oil. The young foreigners sat on the cart, hands tied behind their backs, chained together. Their eyes downcast. Scattered around them were reindeer, seal, and fox skins, along with their implements—spears, harpoons, bows, lassos, and the two odd little boats that no one knew how to use.

Six iron-clad guards stood in a circle around the cart, as if they were guarding a gloomy, mold-colored misfortune.

I saw Henrik push through the colorful, noisy crowd. He approached as if he were going to say his last farewell to the two on their way to the scaffold.

He stopped before them, silent and indecisive. Maybe he was thinking of running away from the whole affair. Leaving them completely to their own fate.

I caught his eye. His gaze was unfathomable and distant. He looked away at once. Searched with his eyes for the horse he was supposed to ride.

I sneaked up to the cart despondently, quietly climbed up and sat right behind the young foreigners. We were in the same boat. The filthy cart was like a pitiful vessel on a huge sea. Just below the surface lurked powerful forces that could pull us under at any time. No one would come to our rescue; each in our own way, we were foreigners. Visible messengers of bad luck amidst the joy.

For the third time, the groomsmen galloped into the courtyard with drumrolls and blunderbuss salutes.

The spokesman roared: "Miss Sofie, are you ready?" His voice was thick with beer.

"Yes!" came a voice softly from the stairs, and there she stood ready in all her glory.

For a moment the noise stopped and a wondering sigh was heard.

She was beautiful.

Blindingly, overwhelmingly, buxomly beautiful.

I had to admit it, even though I saw light against dark, rich against poor, and happiness against catastrophe.

Her eyes shone in triumph. This was her procession, her zenith. Just behind her came Madame Mowinckel, more than ever like a ship under full sail. She bundled her daughter into the waiting bridal carriage, also borrowed for the occasion. It was richly carved and gilded. Adorned with a canopy of embroidered velvet worthy of a queen.

I wondered how many sleepless nights that had cost the poor sailors' widows.

The bridal procession got under way.

The groomsmen rode in front. They swung their beer steins and fired off one salvo after another without restraint.

Behind them came the musicians with their drums, trumpets, and flutes. Then came the bridesmaids and the family, the bridal carriage and the wedding guests, and the wagons full of gifts and dowry, food and drink for the magnificent three-day feast. In the rear came the cart with the young foreigners and me. More than ever I felt cast out and condemned.

The procession crept at a snail's pace through the narrow streets. It progressed slower and slower the closer it came to the marketplace. The whole town was on its feet that morning. Everywhere it was packed with people.

The whole town wanted to make sure they got a look at the wedding gifts and received a mug of the strong beer that Master Mowinckel let flow so freely.

At the edge of the marketplace the procession came to a complete halt. The groomsmen threatened and cajoled people to let the procession through, but the townspeople seemed deaf and blind with anticipation.

It was not all merriment and beauty.

As people cheered the bride, they shook their fists at us on the cart. The curses hailed down, with threats of burning at the stake for all three of us.

I didn't have the strength to be scared. I just stared dully at the rancorous townspeople and wished the whole thing would soon be over—regardless of what happened to me and the foreigners.

We were in the same boat, but we had different fates.

They were sitting close together. They didn't look up, but they whispered to each other. I could hear her doing most of the talking, stroking his hand over and over, as if to give him courage.

I had nobody to give me courage and love.

Across the teeming crowd I saw the marketplace.

It was muddy, though it hadn't rained for a long time.

Stalls in all the colors of the rainbow were jammed up against each other.

They were bulging with wares—lacework and gloves, French wine and Dutch beer, sourdough bread and sweet cakes, live roosters and dead geese, pots and pans, benches and chairs, and everything else that could be sold for money.

On the open square the entertainment had begun. The jugglers with balls and wheels, tightrope walkers, and acrobats. The fire-eater pinched the little dwarf with the big head and the sad eyes, and he screamed louder and louder: "Come closer, good people! Come closer!" The bear tamer whipped away at his old, worn-out bear. Once king of the forest, now a frantic dancing animal, controlled by torture and fear. Peasants hawked well-bred stallions with restless eyes, and billy goats with huge horns. Three men balanced on each other's shoulders next to a group of imperturbable dice players.

It was the way it should be, an exciting market day. But I felt no excitement, only cold loneliness.

"Make way for the bridal procession!"

The booming voice of the best man finally managed to create an opening in the crowd.

"Make way for the bridegroom, the highborn Dr. Abraham!" was the call from the other side of the marketplace. People moved aside as the salvos thundered over their heads.

Horses and goats, angry peasants and excited merchants, jugglers and players were pushed back. The square between the booths was filled by Miss Sofie and Dr. Abraham's magnificent procession.

The beer barrels were rolled out. Everyone had to have a bridal *skål*. The doctor strutted around in a peacock-blue silk suit and embroidered silk hose, his hands glittering with costly rings. The crowd sighed in admiration and the doctor enjoyed it. The beer flowed, and the wedding gifts were displayed. People sighed and bragged even louder. Wonderful! Beautiful! Extraordinary!

I sat stiffly on the cart and felt more outcast than ever before.

My hands were ice-cold and clammy with fear. Soon

[217

it would be time for Miss Sofie's wedding gift, the poor foreigners. If only they did nothing to frighten people and cause the fear of witchcraft to flare up again! If only all would go well, no matter how humiliating it was!

Far away I could hear the doctor bellowing about the wild heathens whom God had looked upon with mercy, who were his property and wedding gift to his sweet dove Miss Sofie, whom she would train like little dogs, and who now for the last time would demonstrate their dark heathen arts . . .

I shook.

Dark heathen arts and demonic witchcraft. They were one and the same to people! Now he had kindled people's worst expectations. How I hated that overdressed man and his dark plans, which I knew all too well!

"Let's see the heathens' black arts!"

The shout rose from many directions, and my tiny hope burst, the hope that people would realize for themselves that the foreigners were lost children among us.

The young man and woman were brutally dragged down off the cart and thrown into the mud at the doctor's feet. The boats and implements followed. The guards stood in a hostile circle around them, as the doctor in an authoritative voice ordered people to stay at a safe distance.

The people obeyed, terrified and ready for a show.

The doctor ordered the guards to remove the chains.

The silence was breathless when the chains clattered to the ground.

They were kneeling in the mud. Their backs were straight. Their faces expressionless.

The shell jewelry shone dully in the sun. I remembered how proudly they had adorned themselves and how glad they were to receive the clothes brushed shiny.

Then I heard the whip scream through the air.

I saw it strike their heads, their backs, their legs. The doctor whipped and whipped like a madman. His face was suddenly purple with excitement.

"Their wills must be broken—devilish pride must be driven out!" he exclaimed. Over and over again.

The crowd chanted: "Crush their will! Drive out the devilish pride!" in time with the whistling whiplashes.

Not a sound came from them, but their faces were contorted in pain. Next to me, Henrik was moaning. In despair, as if the blows were striking him.

He yelled: "Honorable brother-in-law! Is this not a day of happiness? Not a day for punishment and pain! When will you let the people be amused by the foreigners' strange arts?"

The crowd muttered in agreement.

The doctor stopped abruptly, as if wrenched out of a deep dream. He snarled something, so low that only Henrik heard it.

The words ignited a flush in Henrik's face, but the doctor's heavy whip fell to the ground.

The doctor looked around. His eyes met mine, and I froze.

I had just seen the same evil gaze in the bear tamer

who whipped his bear into a senseless rage as the bridal party entered the marketplace. Then one of the bridesmen had asked the bear tamer to restrain himself so that the poor animal could come to its senses. The tamer had looked at them in exactly the same way. Slyly and full of hate.

Henrik was talking to people, friendly and cheerful. About his sister's wonderful wedding day, about all the magnificent wedding gifts, and the rarest gift of all—the foreign children of God from the unknown land across the sea, who wanted so much to show people their great skills as hunters.

Intrigued, people moved cautiously closer.

The young man had prepared himself while Henrik was speaking, and the guards had set up targets.

His implements were different than those I was used to seeing at the marketplace, but never had I seen such accuracy. No one else had either, it seemed, for admiration rose in the crowd for each arrow and each spear that hit its target, no matter where the guards moved the targets.

If there was anything that people in our town knew how to appreciate, it was skills such as these. Old whalers and experienced hunters pressed forward eagerly to study the implements the foreigner handled so masterfully. Just as eagerly he showed them the lassos, the harpoons, the spears and boats, and let the men try them, showed them how the lasso was supposed to lie in the hand. The old whalers were the first to come forward, those who had caught whales and

seals at the dangerous hunting grounds near Spitsbergen. They asked one question after another, and tried
their skill. But no one could hit the targets the way he
could. They tried again, and failed again, and he
laughed good-naturedly and they laughed along with
him.

The people were transformed. Friendly curiosity
flowed toward the two. More and more people dared
to come closer, trying their luck, examining, asking
questions. The women were most interested in the fine
leather embroidery and studied the young woman's
clothing carefully, and she explained willingly.

Eager voices and happy laughter, and over it all
Henrik and the young man talking to each other, each
in his own language.

I felt relief stream warmly through me.

It was almost too good to be true.

If only it would last forever! But imagine what Miss
Sofie would say when all the attention left her? But
there was no need to worry. She was standing in the
middle of a flock of women who were drowning her
in admiring looks and praise. I saw her spin slowly
around so that the gold and silver finery would really
blind them and elicit more envious moans.

Then I suddenly caught sight of the doctor. My
warm feelings vanished like dew in the sunshine.

At the edge of the crowd, behind all those who were
craning their necks to catch a glimpse of the young
man and woman, I could see the doctor whispering
urgently in the bear tamer's ear. The tamer nodded,
giggling.

He was an enormous hulk of a man with malevolent eyes.

I saw him jerk the chain hard so that the dozing bear fell over backwards. With a well-aimed kick he got it to its feet. Then he pushed forward to the foreigners, dragging the wounded bear behind.

People backed away from him and turned solemn and silent at once.

The tamer walked up to the young man and stood with his legs apart, unsteadily, with a challenging look. "You, who know so many strange arts, can probably wrestle a miserable bear," he sneered.

He yanked the chain brutally. The bear choked. Looked up with its yellow eyes. It was a heavy bear. An old, worn-out bear. Its pelt was mangy. Covered with innumerable scars that showed through the sparse, graying fur. Its head and paws were huge. They could probably tear a man to pieces easily, if only the tamer tormented it long enough.

The young man looked watchfully from the tamer to the bear. Henrik whispered something to him, and he nodded slowly and reluctantly.

"Well?" said the doctor, who had finally squeezed his way forward. "Doesn't the wild man dare?"

"Yes, he does," Henrik began. "It's just that—"

"Good!" the doctor cut him off. "Now people are finally going to have some fun for their money!" Suddenly he stuck a flaming pine branch in the bear tamer's hand.

"Here! Give that lazy bear a real jolt! Then it'll be just as wild and mad as this heathen!"

The bear was dozing. It didn't see the pine branch

before it was flaming under its snout. It jerked away, wild with pain.

The pine branch singed it again. Like a raging hornet it raced around the bear, attacking again and again—its paws, its head, its eyes—until the bear was blind with fury and pain. Its terrifying roars went right through marrow and bone. It scrambled to get loose, whirled around after the cruel tormentor with the pine branch, who was howling with laughter.

The wounded roars soon turned to helpless whimpering. Then people stopped laughing.

All at once the young man sprang forward. He struck the pine branch out of the tamer's fist and knocked him over in the mud.

The bear, whimpering in pain, was spinning around in a rage.

The crowd was waiting in breathless suspense.

The young man had taken a few steps back from the bear. He stood completely still, as if waiting for the right moment.

His body was tense like a bow with an arrow notched.

His hands were open.

Then I heard the song. Low, like humming, then louder, as when the wind whistles through the mountaintops. I felt exuberantly happy in the midst of the terrible event taking place.

At first the bear didn't sense anything outside its own pain. It roared and lashed out, with its head weaving back and forth, ready to attack. Its yellow eyes were living fire.

He kept singing, powerful and warm.

[223

People backed up, frightened, and the tamer crawled to safety behind the beer stalls.

But the young man approached the bear, singing.

Then the bear listened, completely still for a moment, with its head tilted. Then it stood up laboriously on its hind feet and opened its enormous embrace. It raised its head and bared its teeth.

He stepped calmly into its mighty embrace.

Bear and man were locked in a hug that only death could loosen. They rocked round and round. Equally proud, equally strong.

The bear's worn-out claws scratched at the man's back, searching for a grip so it could tear him to bits.

He had a hold around the bear's neck. His hands were pitifully small against the mighty head, but they must have been incredibly strong, for the bear staggered and fell over.

Suddenly man and bear lay on the ground, still locked in their embrace, with their heads close together.

He sang to it, low and urgently now.

The bear was still. It was breathing calmly. Now and then it would make a sound. Almost like a cat purring! I thought in amazement.

Its yellow eyes were open and staring as he squeezed.

There was a powerful lurch in the bear's heavy body. Its paws slid down lifeless. Death had loosened the embrace, but not the way any of the people in the marketplace had imagined.

Nor the way I had. My surprise quickly turned to fright as I listened to the muttering around me, and I

thought in confusion: How is it possible for a man to
strangle a bear with his bare hands? Was it possible,
or . . . ? I heard the same thoughts buzzing anxiously
around me.

The young man had knelt down. The head of the
dead bear lay in his lap. He was still singing to it, so
low that it could barely be heard. He sat like this until
she came with the longest spear. He calmly stuck it
into the bear's throat and cut off its huge head.

People were watching breathlessly.

It was still quiet when he stood up with the bear's
head in his arms. Then the silence was broken by a
sharp, triumphant voice I knew all too well:

"Maleficium! Maleficium! God be with us!"

And Pastor Absalon finally had his sincerest wish
fulfilled.

Panic broke out, and people yelled for a burning at
the stake.

"Are you sitting comfortably?"

His voice was happier than she could remember hearing it in a long time. Osuqo hesitated for a moment with her reply.

She couldn't very well just say "yes," since no one would be entirely comfortable, bound tightly with a lasso to the front of a kayak. But there was nothing else on earth she wanted more than just that.

"I'm fine!" she said, and Poq sighed with relief.

It was the darkest time of a summer night.

In front of them lay the mirror-smooth surface of the water, ringed with night-black mountains.

All was quiet.

Only the kayak oar which rhythmically cut through the water broke the silence. At irregular intervals she heard the fish jump. They both rejoiced at the sound. Behind them the lights and the sounds of the foreigners' town disappeared.

Every stroke of the oar made the sounds and the lights fainter.

Every stroke of the oar made the foreigners' power weaker.

Every stroke of the oar let her breathe more freely, more easily.

She was no longer imprisoned in a nightmare.

Now she knew that it would fade someday, like an old evil dream. But it still hurt like an open wound when her thoughts dwelled on it. Especially that terrible day which lay right behind them in the town that was disappearing.

They had fled from that day, and from an infinite number of painful days like it.

Osuqo had never believed in the well-meaning Henrik's babble that one day his people would respect them and treat them like human beings. She didn't believe that they would forget all hatred and foolishness when they got to know Poq and herself.

In her short life she had encountered little hatred, but enough to recognize the dangerous hatred of the foreigners.

It was like a bonfire built of dry branches. Just a tiny spark was enough to light it, and it would burn wildly until it died of its own accord.

She feared their hatred as much as she loathed the cowardice that came with it.

If it had been up to her, the foreigners would never have displayed them at the marketplace. But it was Poq who had made the decision.

She would have refused to eat, refused to speak, refused to obey until the hatred became a poisonous, fatal illness.

But her reason told her that Poq's path was the only way to freedom, though it led through more humiliations, which they could only meet with proud bearing and impenetrable faces.

She had agreed with him so far, but she had refused to feel sympathy and gratitude toward Henrik and the pale girl who was their guard. Poq had spent many hours persuading her to follow their plans. For they were risking a great deal in order to help them, Poq had said. The least he and Osuqo could do was to comply with what they asked.

Mutely she submitted, for she knew that she could never forgive the foreigners for their cruelties. She could never live among them, either. Obediently she did as she was asked. Smiled, listened, looked on with interest as the plans were made. But deep within she knew that however much they crawled and crept, however outlandishly they dressed, or whatever she showed the foreigners, there was no protection against the blind hatred of their captors.

Poq had not given up hope of understanding and forgiveness.

It was the duty of the shaman to penetrate the hidden, to explain the incomprehensible, to reconcile the irreconcilable. He felt that the gods wished the tasks of the shaman to be resolved in that way. But Poq had faced his own limitations that terrible time in the marketplace.

Everything had gone according to Henrik's fragile plan, until Poq faced the tortured bear. He saw a soul more powerless and degraded than his own, and he

[231

acted according to the ancient laws demanding respect for the soul. He had taken the pathetic bear's life and set its soul free to wander. At the same time he had sealed their own fate.

Chaos erupted.

The foreigners, who a moment before had been testing their spears and the harpoon, who had kindly asked questions and listened, were suddenly turned into a howling mob. They smashed the implements to bits and destroyed one of the kayaks. It was only Osuqo's quick-wittedness that had saved the other kayak. She covered it with her own body, and in that way she was dragged out of the marketplace and heaved into the cart while the foreigners howled about devils, punishment, and the stake.

The guards raced through the streets with Poq and her chained to the cart. They took them to a new, final prison, if all went according to Henrik's plan.

The house of the horrible doctor where the wedding was to take place had many dark passageways. The guards threw them into a room and locked the door after they had thrown the pale girl in with them.

The pale girl's eyes were red from crying and her body was shaking as if from fever. Silently she plucked at the white clothes that lay in her lap. The clothes that Osuqo and Poq would be dressed up in, a part of the plan to free them.

Osuqo tried to catch her eye. She longed to say with her eyes what she could never manage to say in their language: "See what you are doing to us! You scorn and trample on everything that has value for us! But we will never be broken. Never will you make us ashamed of our own people! We are richer than you, we love freedom above life!"

But the girl would not meet her eyes. She just stared straight ahead, and Osuqo suddenly recognized her lonely despair. Then she realized that she was looking at the only loser in this terrible game.

Osuqo bent forward, forced the girl to look at her.

Deep in the blue eyes there was a dream. Osuqo suddenly wished that the girl might fulfill her dream.

Gently she took the dress from the girl's hands.

She held it up to the light and saw a profusion of beautiful white flowers.

The girl's eyes were meekly hopeful.

"Yes, it's beautiful," Osuqo said finally. "Very beautiful. Did you . . . ?"

The girl nodded silently.

"Thank you for your generosity," whispered Poq, and Osuqo blushed. "I mean it, Little Sister! In that dress you will be subjected to your last humiliation, but she has done her best to see that the humiliation will be easy to bear."

They had heard the bridal procession outside.

Neighing horses, high-pitched voices, and laughter, drums and salutes.

Henrik came in. His sister was now married to the fat doctor, and the celebration had begun. The guests were already full of food and wine, and Henrik was going to pour more wine for them, he said. The guests had to be senseless, then it would be easy to escape. Soon the last ordeal would begin. She and Poq dressed

as a bridal pair, the young bride's decked-out playthings, who would dance in her honor. Osuqo winced.

"May the gods grant that this is the final humiliation," she whispered.

"You who have endured so much will endure this,"
said Poq quietly.

"Just don't ask me to pity my enemies," she said.

"Then you must learn to distinguish between pity
and the cowardly fawning of a dog," he replied
sternly. "You do know the difference, Little Sister, and
you show it. For you are a true child of our people."

Osuqo had let the girl help her on with the dress.
She stood still as the girl straightened the folds, carefully, meticulously. Calmly, she let the girl comb her
hair and put the wreath of fresh white flowers in place.

The girl took a step back. Her eyes shone with awe
and pride.

Beautifully adorned for humiliation, thought Osuqo
bitterly, but she gently touched the girl's cheek.

The room was large, radiantly lit, full of ruddy-
faced, high-spirited foreign men and women. The air
was suffocatingly hot and stung acridly in her nose.

The heat, the noise, and the hostile anticipation
which struck them made Osuqo feel sick and dizzy.
She thought she would collapse, but they shoved her
out onto the floor, toward the doctor, who was waiting
for them. His face shone red, his voice which roared
something she didn't understand was slurred, and his
legs unsteady. But the eyes which greedily undressed

her were just as cold and evil as she remembered them.

"Poq!" she gasped.

"Do as they ask!" he said. "For the last time, for the last time!"

Like two stiff, white-clad dolls they moved around. The doctor roared something again and laughter resounded. More and more foreigners came out onto the floor, poked at them, patted and pinched them. Osuqo felt hands fumble over her breasts and hips. She thought she was going to throw up. Then the doctor's flaming face was above her and his body pressed against hers. His hands pulled and tore at the beautiful flowers and suddenly she realized what he wanted. Never! It would never happen again! She shoved with all her strength, and the doctor fell over and landed on his back on the banquet table.

He howled like a wounded dog, but before he could get up, the door opened and the guards rushed in. It was not until afterwards that Osuqo found out what they said that so terrified the foreigners. She saw only the confusion, the foreigners who stumbled around, overturned tables, and put out the candles.

Henrik and Poq had dragged her between them over to the pale girl who was waiting outside with horses and a wagon. No one followed them, but they felt the frightening confusion right at their backs.

They jumped into the wagon and quickly put on their own clothes. There lay their kayak, too, and Osuqo heard Poq's sigh of relief.

The horses galloped through the dark, silent streets,

down toward the docks and the brightly lit buildings resounding with song and laughter, past the shops, and out toward the dark headland.

Here the wagon stopped.

"What happened?" asked Poq.

"The bear tamer," answered Henrik darkly. "He was found dead. Strangled by his own bear chain."

"It was . . ." the girl started to say.

"What does it matter what it was?" interrupted Henrik harshly. "All that matters is what they believe killed him, or rather who! You must get away, now! There is nothing else here for you except burning at the stake!"

"He died as he deserved," said Poq stubbornly.

"We agree on that, but no one else in this town will feel the same. They think you are the murderers!"

"But . . ." began Poq.

"Quick!" screamed Henrik. "Don't you understand? You are condemned! They must not get hold of you now! Here's the boat I stole for you," he continued more calmly.

"It should take you far, to Denmark at any rate, or maybe to some other country where they don't know you. You can hide there . . . make a new start . . ."

"We have to go home," said Poq abruptly. "There is no other land but our own. We are strangers in all other places in your world. We need no more proof to know that's the truth."

"But you can't . . ." stammered Henrik.

"We can and we will," said Poq proudly. "We will travel home in our own kayak. Not your foreign boat."

"But . . . that's suicide! Sheer insanity!" gasped Henrik.

Osuqo didn't want to hear any more.

She got the kayak and the lassos out of the wagon. She let the kayak slip gently into the water. She handed the lassos to Poq.

"Will you tie me tightly?" she asked softly.

They reached the mouth of the fjord by the time the sun came up.

The open sea began there. But it was still speckled with islands. The last outposts of the foreigners.

The sea.

Like an open embrace it received them.

The sea.

What they had escaped was the distance between everything dangerous and incomprehensible, and all that was familiar and understandable for which they yearned.

"It is the way of nature itself that the sea is the end of all things. Beyond the sea there is nothing," said Poq. "Did you know that, Osuqo? Did you know how shortsighted the foreigners could be?"

Yes, Osuqo knew. She had heard the foreigners call the People's land Meta Incognita. The foreigners didn't see that the unknown was only unknown to them. They didn't realize either that the sea was the end only for those who couldn't see beyond their own noses.

"Osuqo? This is our bridal procession, did you know that?"

"Yes."

She smiled.

He started to tell the story again, the way he had so often during the last days in the foreign nightmare.

"My grandfather was a great hunter and a stubborn suitor," Poq began. "When he set out to find a wife, he fell deeply in love with a beautiful girl at a settlement far away. But the girl's father didn't think he was good enough, even though the girl begged and pleaded. Then one stormy night Grandfather went to get the girl from the settlement. He tied her to the kayak and they rode the storm home. There they lived happily together."

"It's a good story," said Osuqo. "I always wanted you to come for me on a night full of danger. Now you are fulfilling my wish."

He paddled onward. She knew that he was smiling.

"We will always journey together, do you promise, Poq?"

"Always," he answered solemnly.

The kayak slid faster into the sun-filled embrace.

*I*t's terribly dark here inside the bed-closet,
a close, dense darkness full of vivid pictures I have never seen
and sounds I have never heard.
I can't breathe—can't stop the thoughts
or chase away the images behind my eyelids,
the images of a beautiful land I will never see,
the sound of a wind I will never hear
—like an endless song with no beginning or end
that rises and falls,
from soft humming to a jubilant roar,
the images and the sounds make my heart pound
and the tears burn in my eyes.
I wish it would be gone soon
so I can dream on in peace about the unicorn.

Afterword to the Reader

Books written during the time in which this story is set often had a Foreword to the reader. The authors wanted to explain the book in advance, and also assure the reader that the story was completely true.

I don't think readers need any explanation, but I would like to assure them that this story is true—even though the truth is pieced together from many, many events over a period of more than a hundred years.

Our little Europe has given birth to many explorers and adventurers, who, driven by desire for gold and riches, honor and fame, or in the name of God or science, defied every danger to discover new lands.

The brave Europeans left deep impressions wherever they went. The meetings with foreigners were always disastrous for the country's inhabitants. By force or by argument, their lives were changed. They were thrown into chains and sold as slaves in other parts of the world, annihilated by merciless greed or unknown diseases; they were colonized, Christianized, and civilized. They had to learn what was right and wrong as seen through European eyes, and they were made to feel shame at their skin color, beliefs, and culture, as a christening present from their foreign benefactors.

This is the price that the countless peoples who were "discovered by the white man" are still paying today.

Of the many dark deeds that Europe has on its conscience, the trade in human beings is among the worst of all. From the coasts of Africa, hundreds of thousands were abducted, stuffed into ships, and sold in the slave markets of Europe, naked and robbed of everything— country, family, history. The only thing no one could rob them of was the color of their skin and the yearning for their homeland.

The slave trade reached its peak during the time of the Enlightenment in Europe. Then this misdeed was forbidden. Human worth had triumphed over greed. But the traffic continued long after the prohibition, for there was a lot of money to be made.

In Norway, too, prosperous merchants and shipowners were eagerly engaged in the slave trade, although to a lesser extent than in other countries.

But we have our shame to bear as well, for the hundreds of years of colonization of Samiland, formerly Lapland, and the Dano–Norwegian suppression of Greenland.

We, too, were guilty of abducting people. From the middle 1600s to the middle 1700s, approximately fifty Greenlanders were abducted by ships sailing under the

Norwegian and Danish flag. The captives were shipped to Bergen or Copenhagen, and there they were displayed for the amusement of the king and the people or sent on to learned men in Holland and Germany, who studied their teeth, bone structure, clothing, and language. Some became "civilized," and others were sold to traveling troupes, who exhibited them as strange "wild men."

Many Inuits did not survive the meeting with civilized Norway or Europe. Only a very few ever saw their beautiful cold homeland again.

Many chose death before the ships left the coast of Greenland; others were shot because they tried to defend themselves; and some died in Bergen and Copenhagen from diseases that were unknown to them. Some tried to return across the ocean to Greenland in their fragile kayaks. Of their fate and the fate of others, history tells us nothing.

What did they think and feel, these people who were so brutally torn from family and friends, and who encountered a world they barely knew existed? On this the scholars of the time are silent, for they were only interested in skin and hair, teeth, bone structure, clothing, and language. The writers of history saw the world through the tiny European window. No other point of view existed.

Today we still know little about the many-thousand-year history of the Inuit people in "the Land of the People," Inuit Nunaat. The traces this skilled nomadic people have left behind in history are faint—like soft footprints in heather.

They carried everything with them on their thousand-year wanderings following reindeer, whales, and seals. They carried their history, too, preserved in songs and dances, poems and stories, which the elders guarded and passed on to new generations.

Like most nomadic peoples all over the world, the Inuit people also chose the most practical method of preserving their history and knowledge—oral transmission. But, like many others, the Inuit people also lost their own history when the Norwegian/Danish benefactors started to colonize and civilize in the 1800s. With the new written language, they learned first and foremost to tell others' version of history, and thus much of their own was erased.

But even though exact information about times and places is lost, the songs and poems have kept alive the descriptions of people's relationship to each other and to nature. Despite persistent conversions, the religion of the Inuit people survived long enough to enable the finely balanced relationship between the worlds of human beings and spirits, which only the *angakoqs* (shamans) knew about, to be recorded for posterity.

Thus, the most important aspects of the long history of the Inuit people have been preserved by themselves in living poetry, from generation to generation, and it is the story of how people think and live at the very limits of human existence.

From the history of the Inuit people, it is obvious

that it requires incredible inventiveness and imagination, stamina and patience, love and caring, sacrifice and solidarity. All this in an overpowering nature where a harmonious coexistence between the needs of human beings, animals, and nature is crucial for even the possibility of survival.

These were the people who were abducted from Greenland in the 1600s. So it is not difficult to reconstruct their feelings as they meet the Norway of that day, which has been described more than adequately.

Without the rich sources I have had to draw from, it would not have been possible to write this book. I owe a great debt of thanks to the singers, poets, and storytellers of the Inuit people in Alaska, Canada, and Greenland, and all their intermediaries, from Knud Rasmussen to Ole Jørgensen.

I am also grateful to the captains who kidnapped the Inuits, for their chillingly matter-of-fact descriptions of the events in their logbooks, to the detailed descriptions, by Hans Egede and a multitude of others, of the meaningless lives of "the deranged wild men" without the blessings of civilization. Without their help, I would never have been able to lend credibility to that era's men of power.

This is the story of a clash of cultures. There is always a clash between different ways of organizing life. Yesterday, as well as today, it is equally a meeting of reason and unreason.

Reason listens openly and without prejudice, and admits mistakes. Unreason always wants to use power to enforce injustice.

Today—as well as yesterday.

The author
Oslo
March 15, 1987